Szymon
Szechter
A Stolen
Biography

Szymon Szechter

A STOLEN
BIOGRAPHY

TRANSLATED BY
FRANCES CARROLL
AND NINA KARSOV

Nina Karsov
London

United States distributor
DUFOUR EDITIONS, INC.
Booksellers and Publishers
Chester Springs, PA 19425
215-458-5005

First published in Great Britain in 1983
by **Nina Karsov**
28 Lanacre Avenue, London NW9 5FN

Second edition (with illustrations added) published in 1985

Originally published in Polish as *Czas zatrzymany do wyjaśnienia*
(**Kontra**, London 1972; second edition 1983)

British Library Cataloguing in Publication Data

Szechter, Szymon
    A stolen biography. − 2nd ed.
    I. Title   II. Czas zatrzymany do wyjaśnienia. *English*
    891.8'537 [F]   PG7178.Z35

    ISBN 0-907652-16-6

Library of Congress Catalogue Card Number 84-70938

Cover and illustrations by Andrzej Krauze

Reproduced from copy supplied,
printed and bound in Great Britain
by Billing and Sons Limited, Worcester

CONTENTS

The Broken Clock   7
The New Secretary   19
David and Goliath   28
The New Chairman   36
Inspiration   43
Maryla   52
The Stolen Biography   57
The Manuscript Returned   69
The Aviary   76
Goldberg   85
Where Do All These Jews Come From?   94
Zionist   101
Chapter Thirteen   110
Two Homelands   111
California   123
The Press Lies   137
The Promise   146
Time Arrested   155
The Next to Last   169
The Welcome   170

Chapter 1
THE BROKEN CLOCK

The authors of this story are little Jozek, who grew up to be big Jozef, and big Jozef, who was once little Jozek. Besides these two, there are others involved in the story, among them the Critic, who always has some reservations.

'Well, not reservations as yet, but questions. The first question is how can Jozek write a story with Jozef when they have never, nor could have ever, seen each other, for when Jozek was little, Jozef did not yet exist, and when he did, little Jozek was no longer there because he had grown up to be big Jozef? That is just not possible!'

'Yes it is, and it's very simple,' said Jozek. 'All you have to do is break the clock on the kitchen wall.'

'That is,' said Jozef, 'do away with time.'

'Very well,' the Critic again interrupted, 'but how can you describe events? Surely they must be bound to time?'

'Events, yes, but not writers if they don't want to be separated.'

'Well,' said the Critic, 'we'll see. For the moment, however, I'm going to leave you as I consider this rubbish unworthy of my interest.'

'Fine, then we can begin.'

I'm almost ten years old and I'm in the fourth grade...

'Careful, Jozek, you've made a blot.'

'It's not my fault. I always make blots when someone is standing over me. Now, where was I? Oh, yes...'

... I'm in the fourth grade of Maria Konopnicka Primary School. Our teacher had us write a composition for homework on 'Why I like to read books', and I wrote that I like to read books when I'm sick and my mother makes me stay in bed, but mostly I like to play in our yard. Our teacher read my composition aloud and the whole class laughed. Then the teacher said that I was featherbrained and that nothing good would come of me and that books were wasted on me. I got mad at her, and at the class too because they laughed at me, so when we had to write a composition on 'What I would like to be when I grow up', I wrote that I would like to be a writer so I could write a book about our yard that all grown-ups would have to read. The teacher did not read this composition aloud. She preferred to read Heniek's, who wrote that he wanted to be a soldier and defend our homeland. I started to laugh, but nobody else laughed and the teacher sent me out of the room. I wandered around the hall for a while, and met you and said I wanted to write about our yard, only I didn't know how to begin.

'Why don't you write a bit? I'm getting tired.'

'All right,' said Jozef, 'I'll try, and you take a rest.'

... Every tenement has a yard. Our yard, however, is unusual, because one can go from it straight into the next tenement's yard through a short, narrow passage...

'I don't like the way you write. It's not just any old passage, but a real pass of death.'

... War was continually waged over this pass, and during occasional brief truces there were interyard peeing contests...

'Maybe we shouldn't mention that. It was a long time ago, still in the second grade.'

Big Jozef looked at little Jozek, who was peering intently at his toe-caps.

'We are not going to conceal it,' he said. 'Grown-ups also pee and it would be better for grown-ups to learn from children how to compete in peeing than for children to learn from grown-ups how to knock each other's teeth out.'

... And it happened that the uncontested peeing champion on both sides of the pass was Jozek. He peed highest and furthest. For this he was respected and envied very much, but what gave Jozek the right to feel proud caused Heniek a lot of misery. Heniek was always last, not only in the competitions but also during training. This was not surprising, since when the time for the competition came, Heniek couldn't pee. 'He's a girl, maybe' they said, and pulled his trousers down to see if he really had one. 'He does,' said Staszek, 'but it's a Jewish one!' Jozek didn't understand and asked, 'What do you mean "a Jewish one"?' 'I mean a snipped one. You can always tell a Jew that way.' Jozek then realized what an advantage he had over that shitty old Heniek.

The bell rang and it was time to run out to the play-ground. The teacher left the classroom and she might have seen Jozek and Jozef sitting on the stairs, writing something, so Jozek said,

'You know, I'd better go for my break. Let's meet again tomorrow, but not at school. Come to our yard. I'll wait for you there.' And he ran off.

'Allow me,' said the Critic and he approached Jozef, 'I did have a sincere wish not to interfere in your affairs, but my feeling of responsibility for the written word obliges me to warn you, my dear colleague, against the consequences of slandering our children. Are you aware of the fact that, contrary to historical truth, you are accusing them of racism? If you do not delete that scene about the peeing, you will be dropped from the Writers' Union and...'

'I understand, but you see, that's how it really was. Little Jozek...'

'Little Jozek is a hooligan, from whom no good will ever come.'

'But if so, maybe I shouldn't write about this either,' and Jozef led the Critic to a grey, three-storey tenement house. They went in through the front entry and turned right, went up the stairs to the first floor and came out on to the balcony which surrounded the yard on three sides. They walked along the balcony, passing the doors of a few flats, one of which was Jozek's, until they reached the end, where they went into the toilet used by all the tenants on that floor. On the inside of the door someone had scrawled in chalk: JEW HENIEK.

'Tch-tch, that's a nice story,' said the Critic.

And Jozef eased open the toilet door just enough to see what was happening not only on the balcony but in Jozek's flat, next to the toilet. Heniek's mother, Mrs. Mazurkiewicz, was walking along the balcony. She came to Jozek's door, knocked vigorously, and without waiting for the 'come in', went in, leaving the door open behind her. At the sight of the unexpected guest, Jozek's mother shooed her son out of the room, while his father bowed to Mrs. Mazurkiewicz and kissed her hand. Mrs. Mazurkiewicz did not offer her hand to Jozek's mother, nor did she sit in the chair which Jozek's father had politely drawn up for her. Without any preliminaries, she announced that she had come to express her deep indignation because of Jozek's bad behaviour, let us not mince words, his scandalous act.

'Our family,' began Mrs. Mazurkiewicz with great feeling, 'is well-known for its spirit of tolerance and humanity. Our son Henryk has been brought up in the best patriotic tradition, thanks to which he could have had quite a beneficial influence on your son. What's more, we welcome Israelites in our home — like the Baruchs — and Mr. Wilhelm Kugelman, the parliamentary candidate, sends season's greetings every year to Mr. Mazurkiewicz. However, your son has written on the, forgive me, I am forced to use such a word, on the lavatory door, a disgusting insult aimed at the good name of our family. Allow me,' Mrs. Mazurkiewicz made a sign with her hand, stepped out on to the balcony and thrust open the toilet door with such energy that Jozef and the Critic barely had time to jump aside and save their noses. Jozek's father followed Mrs. Mazurkiewicz in. 'There! Would you please read and comment on the work of your son.' Jozek's father took a handkerchief out of his pocket and began to rub out the writing. 'Very good,' said Mrs. Mazurkiewicz, 'but you, and your wife as well, of course,' — Jozek's mother had also edged her way into the toilet and it had become very crowded — 'should not just punish your son severely — that will not suffice, for it is most important that a child be made

11

aware from its earliest years of its religious and national origin. I'm sure you have both understood me,' Mrs. Mazurkiewicz added and she extended two fingers to Jozek's father.

Deeply ashamed, he bowed low, timidly kissed her outstretched hand, and escorted her back to the door.

'I would advise you not to write about this either. What does it matter that this hooligan you're moulding into the hero of your story was only in the second grade at that time and could barely spell — his excessive behaviour could still work against you, believe you me,' said the Critic and followed Mrs. Mazurkiewicz out.

Jozef did not budge, although he had no reason to remain, knowing well what would happen in a moment. He would like to have helped little Jozek very much, for Jozek had nothing pleasant to face, but the clock — the one hanging on the kitchen wall — would not go backwards. So he waited for a moment until Jozek's mother, and then his father, returned to the flat, and then he peeped through the keyhole. Little Jozek was standing in the middle of the kitchen, biting his fingernails.

'Do you know who was here a minute ago?' asked his mother.

'And what she told us, you whelp?!' added his father.

'I know,' said Jozek, 'but it's true!'

'It's good that you owned up at once, Jozek,' said his mother, pleased.

'Wait a minute!' his father exclaimed. 'What's true, you little wretch?!' His hand reached down for his belt and undid the buckle, but Jozek's mother shielded the boy.

Jozek must have felt safer, for he cried out, 'It's true, isn't it? Heniek is a Jew!'

'You dummy!' roared his father, 'and what are you then?! Do you know what you are?!'

12

'Not like that,' Jozek's mother put in gently,'not like that. You heard what Mrs. Mazurkiewicz said. You must explain things to the boy, don't you see, explain, but here you are shouting.'

His father sat down and started more calmly: 'Tell me, Jozek, do you know who you are? who I am? your mother?'

Jozek was silent.

'It's we who are Jews.'

'No!' shouted Jozek. 'I'm not a Jew! Believe me, Papa, I'm not!' He ran to the door and out on to the balcony. He did not even notice Jozef as he rushed out into the yard.

Jozef followed after him. He walked slowly, passed the door of the Mazurkiewiczes and went down the stairs, but did not turn right into the yard. He stood for a moment in the entry, lit a cigarette (because he was extremely agitated) and then went out to the street.

'I shouldn't really blame myself,' he said to himself. 'I had no influence on what happened. The clock on the kitchen wall has been broken and doesn't go, that's true, but rivers still flow, people die, children grow up. I too have grown up, and I'm different now. I have a right to be different. I always was different.'

He threw away his unfinished cigarette, boarded a tram, and went to Party House, where the Secretary was waiting for him.

'Comrade Potoczek,' he said, 'we are assigning you to a responsible post. We have confidence in you...'

The Secretary went on speaking, but Jozef was not listening. He waited until the Secretary finished, then sat down by a table in the waiting room and began to fill out a questionnaire. In the box marked 'mother', instead of Rachel, he wrote 'Rozalia née Mickiewicz', exactly as it was on his birth certificate made out during

13

the Occupation, and as he had written ever since. In the box marked 'father', instead of Jakub Hirszfeld, he wrote 'Jan Potoczek', also in accordance with the false certificate and with what he had been writing for many years. In the box marked 'ethnic origin', Jozef, as always, did not write the truth. But today, as he was handing back the completed questionnaire, it seemed to him that the Secretary was smiling somewhat strangely.

'I am obliged to warn you again, my dear colleague,' said the Critic. 'The Comrade Secretary has confidence in you, and yet all the while you... well, first this broken clock, a naive attempt to fiddle with time, with time that is working in our favour and in that of our party; next this immoral peeing scene with its racist under-tones, then the same old story with the questionnaire, and now this implication of our Party Secretary's 'mysterious smile'. No, Comrade Potoczek, if I were you I would think it all over and submit a self-criticism as fast as I could, and above all I would forego associating with this young hooligan and writing this, to put it mildly, foolish story. I will go further and assert that if you do not do this yourself, I will carry out the duty of a Party member on your behalf.'

'No, not yet,' replied Jozef. 'I couldn't do that now. They would start asking me why I didn't do it earlier, why I concealed it from the Party. And what could I say to them? No, not now. First I will complete the story with Jozek, publish it, receive an award, and then no one will ask questions. A writer can do this. A mere Party member, no, but a writer, whose creative work — not some old questionnaire, but creative work — is an expression of truth, yes, he has a right to do this. The Critic wanted to say something more, but he was summoned by the Secretary.

Jozef went home, and on the way thought 'I must be

'Comrade Potoczek,' he said,
'we are assigning you to a responsible post' (page 13)

more careful and warn Jozek that our meetings must somehow be concealed from the Critic. But where can we hide the manuscript? Hmm... What about inside the broken clock? Yes, that's a wonderful idea!'

And instead of going home, Jozef went back to Jozek's flat. He peered inside through a crack in the door and, having convinced himself that there was no one in the kitchen, went in and stuffed the handwritten sheets into the clock where the cuckoo was perched — bored because the clock had been broken and it could not cuckoo time. Jozef wanted a drink of water and had already reached for a cup when something stirred in the next room and he left quickly, ran along the balcony, and just managed to get out on to the street, as Szymonowa locked the big wooden doors because it was already ten o'clock, and at that time decent people were in bed.

Jozek had been asleep for a long time now, and Rachel and Jakub were lying next to each other talking in undertones. How do we know this? There are various kinds of stories — good stories, bad stories, and so-so stories, interesting and boring — but there are also those in which something is missing. What? Well, no one actually knows what, neither the writer nor the reader, but please do not confuse the latter with the critic: he always knows everything. And so, in the story by the two Jozefs, something would have been missing — yes, the conversation between Jakub and Rachel would have been missing, if the cuckoo had not been there, for who else would have written down, ... sorry, cuckooed out their conversation but that bored bird. Jozek, as we know, was already asleep, and big Jozef was waiting at the stop for the night tram to take him home at last.

Jakub was patiently explaining to Rachel that, of course, he was not going to feel guilty about this. True, their only son was growing up to be a Goy, and what is more, an anti-Semite, but can one blame a father for that? When he must earn a bit of bread for the whole family, pay the rent, pay for clothes — and could he, a master barber, appear before his clients dressed like a tramp? — and pay the washerwoman, too, and even feed her during work, so as to save the strength and good health of his wife, and when he must toil from morning to night day in and day out, and most of all before Sundays, on Saturdays, and before feast-days, then how can he concern himself with bringing up their son? Rachel, that's a different matter — she's home all day, she has a lot of work to do, that's true, but...

Rachel tried to defend herself: And is it her fault that she can hardly read or write? And as for sending Jozek not to a Jewish school but to a Goyish one, well, wasn't it Jakub himself who decided that? 'My son does not have to be Jewish,' surely Jakub would remember what he had said, 'Enough that I am Jewish and have a Jewish father-in-law.'

At the very mention of his father-in-law Jakub turned away sharply from Rachel and spat. 'Agh! Devil take him! May he squander all his fortune on the doctors! He would eat his own shit from underneath him while his daughter, naked, in a night-dress, he threw out of his house, because it was not for money but for love that she wanted to marry him, Jakub, poor it is true, but honest!'

Rachel did not correct Jakub, for what sense would it make to remind him that it was not her father who had thrown her out, but she herself who had left home? True, her father did not want to agree to her marriage with Jakub, but it was not because of the money. 'You, Rachel,' he said, 'you want to bring shame on your family. Who could imagine that a Jewish girl from a good home should marry some schmuck who shaves not just Goyish, but even Jewish beards, and on the holy Sabbath, too.' Nor, to the cuckoo's surprise, did Rachel remind her husband that he had been a Red, but, praise be to God, had broken off with those devils after having spent a week in a police cell. But, that Jakub had forbidden her to speak Yiddish in front of the child — that Rachel did say. Surely Jakub would not deny that now?

And Jakub did not deny it. He simply stated that it would be necessary to explain everything to Jozek once more, patiently and wisely. Rachel agreed with Jakub but thought that he was too nervous to do it, that better someone else should talk to the boy.

'Who else? Not his own father, and not his mother because, as she says, she would not be suitable for that, so who then? Perhaps Israel Mickiewicz, that great rabbi, your father, may his bones...'

'Best of all,' said Rachel, 'that it should be done by Jozek's teacher, the one who teaches him religion.'

Jakub leapt up in the bed as if someone had unexpectedly poured scalding hot water over him.

'Quiet or you'll wake up Jozek,' hissed Rachel.

But Jakub could not stop himself from exclaiming, 'That fool? He teaches my son religion and has not even taught him that he is a Jew! What do they pay him money for! I must go and see him tomorrow...!'

What followed the cuckoo did not record because it had become very tired, wiped the ink off its beak and fallen asleep immediately.

Jozef was also asleep by now, and he dreamed that he was at a meeting at which the Critic was expelled from the Party.

Chapter 2
THE NEW SECRETARY

Grown-ups do not like wars, not because they have to kill, but because they could die or lose the war. And grown-ups do not like it when children play at war, even though they themselves taught them how. So it was not strange that Szymonowa from our yard and Karolowa from the next collected enough money from the tenants to hire a bricklayer who brought some bricks and mortar in a wheelbarrow and divided up the pass of death with a wall a little higher than a normal grown-up to prevent the children from playing at war. But this cunning plan did not succeed. True, the land war ceased — the armed assaults on the enemy camp ended, as did the capture of prisoners of war, bayonet charges, and the heroic defence of the standards — but in its place air war broke out. Pieces of brick which the bricklayer had neglected to sweep away were flying in both directions, along with stones, lumps of earth, and even bottles. And again Jozek distinguished himself, this time as the hurler of projectiles.

Grown-ups are naive when they think it is enough to erect a boundary and there will be no war. This is what Szymonowa and Karolowa believed, for otherwise they would not have thought up this wall and, when the wall didn't work, they would not have ordered a wire netting to be fixed along the top of the wall, reaching half-way up to the second floor. Grown-ups cannot understand that the harder it gets to cross a frontier, the more sophisticated and effective become the means of waging war, and the wider its range. No one, not even Jozek, was capable of hurling projectiles over this wire netting, so the hostile forces began to arm themselves with catapults. Nor was anyone, apart from Szymonowa and Karolowa, to blame that the rules of waging war were broken, that panes were gone in the neutral territory, and bruises appeared, not so much among the soldiers, as among the toddlers not subject to mobilization who were wandering about on the balconies — though, of course, nobody wanted this to happen.

The first to declare that he would not fight in such a war was Jozek. And he said this not because he regretted the windows and the wailing toddlers, not at all. Jozek simply could not come to terms with the fact that the best at catapulting was Heniek. He had got a catapult from somewhere, not one with a wooden fork and an elastic taken from a girl's knickers, but one with a metal fork and real, thick rubber which was difficult to stretch and which therefore sent its projectile highest and furthest. Heniek showed off his catapult like a real general and would not allow anybody else to try it except Staszek. Jozek only once said, 'give it to me; I want a try.'

'I'm not giving it to a Jew,' answered Heniek and, as he knew what was coming to him for this 'Jew', tried to get away but didn't quite make it. Jozek punched him in the ear, tripped him, and Heniek fell, bawling so that the whole tenement heard him.

Mrs. Mazurkiewicz ran up and Jozek made off. No, not because he was a coward and afraid of Mrs. Mazurkiewicz. He made off because he did not like those jangling grown-ups. Perhaps Mrs. Mazurkiewicz did not know this, as she yelled after Jozek, 'You coward, you're afraid to take your medicine! You caught him unawares, you sneak!' And to Staszek, who'd been present throughout, she said, 'how could you let this happen, you, a Legionnaire's son? How could you let your friend get beaten up?'

Staszek was silent. Well, was he perhaps to explain to Mrs. Mazurkiewicz that he was not a grown-up, and did not, as grown-ups did, meddle in other people's affairs? If Jozek really had caught Heniek unawares as Mrs. Mazurkiewicz had yelled, and not alone, then maybe he would have stood up for Heniek. But when it was one against one, Staszek was not the sort to interfere.

Mrs. Mazurkiewicz took Heniek with her out of the yard and went off. On the balcony they came across Staszek's father. He was standing in the doorway of his flat with a mug of beer in his hand, probably drawn outside by the shouting.

'It's beyond belief that your son, the son of a Legionnaire,' said Mrs. Mazurkiewicz, 'did not defend his friend, and allowed that other one, that little...'

Staszek's father turned his back to her: 'She's not the one to teach me — first let her teach her old man to flush the toilet,' and he slammed the door behind him.

'You are coming along rather nicely,' said the Critic to Jozef as they were walking up to the first floor. 'Disavowal of Legionnaire traditions in our literature is very much the thing today. Only... well, you see, my dear colleague, again you are kindling in your readers' minds the phenomenon of an anti-Semitism that is over and done with. You know, it would be best if all that were completely forgotten, otherwise...'

Jozef was not listening to what the Critic was saying next, as he had just noticed Jozek who had run up to them, said his customary 'Hi!' and dragged Jozef off by the sleeve.

They turned back and went into the corner café for an ice cream. Jozek ordered a cone for himself and a dish for Jozef. He licked his ice cream without looking at Jozef. And, on the whole, he seemed out of sorts. At last he said, 'I don't like this Critic dogging you all the time.' He said this not out of jealousy, but because he did not like being nagged.

'I can't stand it either,' Jozef replied.

'Then why are you always whispering together? Make him go away and that's all.'

'I can't really. You see, he's my colleague,' Jozef explained. 'We both belong to the Writers' Union, and from time to time we have to deal with each other about certain matters, and it wouldn't be fitting...'

'Rubbish!' exclaimed Jozek. 'Take Heniek for instance: we live in the same tenement, play in the same yard, go to the same class, even sit in the same row, and so what? That doesn't stop me from punching him in the jaw from time to time to get him out of my hair.'

22

Jozef smiled, thought for a minute, and said nothing to that. He only asked, 'Do you want to write today?'

'Yes.'

'Well then, run home and get our manuscript. I hid it in the clock.'

'In the clock? What a hiding place! I'll find a safer one; and anyway, it would be better off with me than with you.'

'Why?' Jozef was curious.

'Because I'm not sure you won't go and show it to that Critic,' and before Jozef could answer, little Jozek had run out to get the manuscript.

An hour or more passed and little Jozek did not come back. Indeed, something had happened which no one could have foreseen. In the kitchen of Jozek's flat, with the manuscript in front of him, sat the Critic. He was talking with the cuckoo — that is, he was asking it something and it was cuckooing something back. When they saw Jozek, they became silent. Then the cuckoo hopped back into the broken clock, and the Critic got up and went off, leaving the manuscript on the table. Jozek barely had time to take it away before his father came in and said,

'Tomorrow I'm going to talk to your religion teacher about you.'

'We aren't having religion tomorrow.'

'Don't lie to me. I saw it on your school schedule and I know you have it last period.'

Jozek also knew, but was not too keen on his father meeting the teacher. Religion was always last period, and, although the end of the year was coming, Jozek had not yet been to a single religion class. And now, what bad luck. Papa would come to school and find out everything.

'As you wish, Papa; if you want to come, then come,

but our religion teacher is sick,' Jozek tried to wriggle out of it.

'We will see,' said his father and went into the next room to take a nap.

Then Mama came back from shopping, gave them dinner, and Jozek completely forgot that big Jozef was waiting for him at the café.

And at Party House, the Secretary was saying to the Critic, '... But that, Comrade, was a period of errors which we must now make up for. Our Party, as you know, does not conceal that from society, and therein lies its strength. Our struggle with the class enemy has been a life and death struggle. The line of battle was clearly marked out: whoever was not with us was against us. But now it is different. We must win the undecided over to our side too, even if it means shutting our eyes to their old habits which have not yet been eradicated; patiently, step by step, contenting ourselves with small successes, we must proceed with perseverance towards our established aim, and that aim is the new man. And for this work we need people who are popular in society or, at least, unknown in the previous period, but tested and proven worthy of our confidence. You understand me, Comrade, don't you? Let us take, for example, Potoczek...' Here the Secretary reached for a file and started to take some papers out of it.

The Critic, who was seated at a desk opposite the Secretary, raised himself up a little, leaned over the papers to see them better and pointed to a paper with a lot of writing on it. 'You are probably looking for this, Comrade Secretary; I recognize my own handwriting. It is my very report on the writer Potoczek.'

'Yes,' said the Secretary, 'it is your report. But I must stress that the conclusions which you draw suggest certain reservations.'

24

And at Party House,
the Secretary was saying to the Critic (page 24)

'Why is that!' the Critic exclaimed. 'They have never done so in the past.'

'That is true,' the Secretary replied calmly. 'On the contrary, we have relied upon them, even made use of them when we were taking our resolutions at Party House, but times have changed and...'

'I understand,' the Critic interrupted, 'they are perhaps a little too harsh. I'll alter them immediately.'

'That won't be necessary. We merely would like you, without blunting your Party vigilance for a moment, to lay stress in your work not so much on the class struggle, as on uniting all society around our Party.' The Secretary put the papers back in the file. 'Now, Comrade, some personal matters. Potoczek, in our opinion, would not be bad as Secretary of our Party branch in the Writers' Union, and you...'

The Critic beamed and even drew himself up to attention, for if Potoczek were to be the Secretary, then surely he would be Chairman of the Union.

'... and you,' the Secretary repeated slowly, 'will now be his deputy.'

The Critic sank back into his chair and had to control himself very hard so as not to let the Secretary see what this decision meant to him. Then he said, 'I'm sorry, Comrade Secretary, but Potoczek is now writing a story which...'

'Ye-e-es?' said the Secretary.

'Yes!' the Critic could not hold back.

And the Secretary, who was in the habit of speaking very slowly, went on, 'we hope that story will be useful to our Party.'

And Jozef, who could not wait for Jozek any longer because the café was closing, got into a taxi and drove off to the Writers' Union for a Party meeting.

It had just started when Jozef entered the hall. He sat

against the wall by the window and was beginning to think over what Jozek had said to him today, when suddenly he heard his own name.

'Comrade Potoczek,' the Critic was speaking from behind the platform table, 'is, in my opinion, and I am sure I am not mistaken when I say in the opinion of my colleagues as well, the most fitting amongst us to assume the position of Secretary of our organization. As for me,' he continued, pretending that he was moved, 'I am fully aware that I have made many errors for which I must answer.'

As he was saying this, somebody thrust into Jozef's hand a note folded four times. Jozef unfolded it and read: 'Propose the Comrade Critic as your deputy.' He stood up and asked to speak.

'I would like to thank you all,' he said, 'for the honour bestowed upon me. I will endeavour not to shake the confidence which has been placed in me by our Party and, in order to be equal to my task, I would like to request,' and here he turned to the Critic, 'that the Comrade accept the position of Deputy. The Comrade's experience...'

He went on, but those present drowned his words with loud clapping. They were pleased by the noble gesture of the new Secretary who had asked his rival, known to be so by everyone, to work with him.

And little Jozek, who was now in bed, called out something in his sleep, for he saw that the Critic was writing a composition for Heniek.

Chapter 3
DAVID AND GOLIATH

Jozek crept into class, closed the door quietly behind him, and sat down in the back row. The teacher was just blowing his nose with a large chequered handkerchief and did not notice Jozek come in. He folded his handkerchief back into his pocket and said, 'I think I have caught this cold from you, Goldberg. You always have a runny nose, but I can't deny myself the pleasure of giving you a kiss — it always seems to me that you are a little girl. However, there will be no kissing today, so don't come near me. And no top mark either.'

Having said this he blew his nose again, and then put on his glasses and started reading something about David and Goliath. Jozek was not listening. He looked around the class and was very surprised that so many children went to religion. He only started listening when the teacher said that David was a Jewish king and Goliath a Philistine.

'And it came to pass, when the Philistine arose, and came and drew nigh to meet David, that David hasted, and ran toward the army to meet the Philistine. And David put his hand in his bag, and took thence a stone, and slang it, and smote the Philistine in his forehead, that the stone sunk into his forehead; and he fell upon his face to the earth. So David prevailed over the Philistine with a sling and with a stone, and smote the Philistine, and slew him; but there was no sword in the hand of David.'

'This David,' thought Jozek, 'is just like that shithead Heniek, just shifty. Too chicken to fight with a sword.'

And Jozek did not listen to what came next. He took out his last ham roll, leaned forward so as not to be seen, and began to eat, but the teacher noticed him because his pencil case fell to the floor with a clatter.

'And you, who are you, my little doll?' asked the teacher. 'What's your name and how did you come to be here?'

'Hirszfeld, sir, Jozek Hirszfeld,' mumbled Jozek.

'Hirszfeld? Just a minute,' and the teacher began to look for something in his notebook. 'Ah, I've got you. The mule has come down to the cart, has it? Eh? And where has it been wandering about until now, eh?'

'Well, my head hurt a little bit, and I was sick for a little bit,' muttered Jozek.

'Sore head, sore finger — sore excuse, eh? Come here, my pretty little Esther.'

Why the teacher called him Esther, Jozek did not know, but he got up from his desk and the whole class laughed.

'Come here and let me give you a kiss, princess.'

Jozek stopped short. He said that he had the flu and a cough, and went back to his place. He did not like it when grown-ups kissed him. The teacher got up from his desk and was about to go after Jozek, but the bell rang and the children jumped up from their desks and crowded the aisle, and Jozek, who sat nearest the door, ran out into the corridor, straight into his father.

'Oh, it's you, Papa. How are you?'

'Yes, it's me, you little devil. Well, did you have religion?'

'No, there wasn't any. I told you, the teacher is sick.'

And Jozek, with a wink at Goldberg, said, 'my father's come to see our religion teacher. I've told him the teacher's sick and there was no class, but he doesn't believe me. Tell him I'm telling the truth.'

Goldberg bowed politely to Jakub and nodded his head, which meant that Jozek had told the truth, and together the three of them started to edge towards the exit. When Jozek was sure that his father would not come back he called to his father that he had an extra gym class, and together with Goldberg he ducked under the stairs just next to the cloakroom.

'I've been looking for you everywhere,' said the Critic and he walked up to Jozek. 'Come on, I'll treat you to an ice cream, and I'll tell you something.'

'I don't really want any ice cream. I've got to...' He tried to escape but the Critic seized him by the arm.

'Wait, I want to talk to you. Tell me, do you like Jozef a lot?'

Jozek was silent.

'You are silent, so you like him. I expected that. If you really do like him then you should understand that your too frequent meetings do not foster the creative work of your friend. You probably know already that

Jozef has been specially honoured; he has become Secretary and... well, how can I explain it to you? You see, not only children have a future before them, but adults as well, and fortune does not favour everybody, so the chance it has given Jozef should not be taken away from him by you, Jozef's friend. Surely you understand me?'

Jozek was silent.

'You are silent, so you do understand and agree with me. That's very good. You should also start thinking of yourself; it's high time. You are now in the fourth grade. The school year is coming to an end, and in a few months you will take your exams for grammar school. Your future depends on that. You should study hard and come to grips with your sums, for example, since they seem to escape you. You should put off writing the story until later, and your meetings with Jozef as well, ah yes... I've just remembered. I left your manuscript in the kitchen on the table; I wouldn't want it to get lost anywhere...'

'You don't have to worry,' Jozek muttered quietly.

'What did you say? I didn't hear you.'

'Nothing,' Jozek grunted.

'And I would like you from time to time to let me read what you have written. As you know, I am a critic, which means that it is my duty to help writers in their creative efforts.'

'Get it if you want it,' said Jozek.

'Thank you for your permission, but I don't know where you keep it.'

'With Satan in his kennel!' And, taking advantage of the Critic's astonishment, Jozek pulled his hand away and ran off.

'Hm, you aren't doing so badly,' said the Bearded Poet as he came into the office where Jozef was working.

'A waiting room, even a Not Unattractive Secretary —
"Please wait. The Comrade Secretary is on the phone; he
will see you in a moment" — period furniture, three tele-
phones, an iron safe just like in a bank, a picture of our
saint on the wall, as if it were in a church... mm... mm...
But that's not what troubles me, Comrade Sir; I have
dragged myself here, my old friend, to congratulate you
on your latest article. I read it, rubbed my eyes, spat
a few times. I simply couldn't get over it: there was
once a guy named Potoczek, not a bad sort of fellow
really, and suddenly he doesn't exist anymore. Simply
doesn't exist. Just like that. No, my friend, you can
speak in the name of the whole Union as much as you
like, you may consider it right to close down our journal,
and you can bark as loud as you want at... wait a minute,
what was it you wrote? — ah yes, at hooligans... But in
my name? — no, you will not be speaking in my name.
Here, take back your toy, the game's over.'

The Bearded Poet took his still new Party membership card out of his pocket and put it on the table and,
before Jozef could say a word, he had gone, slamming
the door behind him.

'The devil take him,' said the Critic who came in a
moment later. 'I never trusted him very much.'

Jozef, who was standing by the window, took one
look at the Critic and could not help exclaiming: 'Whatever happened to you, my dear friend?!'

The Critic's cheeks, forehead, nose, chin and hands
were all covered with pink band-aids.

'The merest trifle,' he said, 'my razor happened to
be dull.'

Jozef smiled, but in a way that the Critic would not
notice. 'A bright little fellow, my Jozek; he knew who
to trust with the manuscript,' he thought.

Jozek knew. Not some silly cuckoo-informer who

'... it is my duty to help writers in their creative efforts'
(page 31)

would cuckoo everything out to everyone whether asked for it or not, but Satan.

Satan, an enormous dog, lived in a wooden kennel almost directly opposite Jozek's tenement. During the day he was tied up by a chain, and at night he roamed around the small garden and guarded the villa — the local court-room now, but at one time the home of a professor who had been locked up as a reactionary. Satan was Jozek's friend. He did not pry into the manuscript which Jozek had entrusted to him, for he was not inquisitive like the cuckoo, and, on the whole, disliked those who were. And what is more, he could not be bribed. He would not touch the sausage that the Critic tried to give him, and even roughed him up a little. Jozek watched from his hiding place, giggling.

Jozef pretended he believed all that about the razor, and he and the Critic sat at the table to edit what the Critic had written about literature for children and youth.

'I've found you at last.' Jozek burst like a bomb into the room.

'I'm very busy, Jozek, hold on a minute.'

But the Critic got up, adjusted a band-aid on his chin, and said, 'we'll finish it later, dear colleague,' and went out.

'I don't like it here.'

'Well, let's go and have some cakes then,' Jozef suggested.

'You can't write in a café either, the park's the best place,' said Jozek.

But there was no bench free in the park, so they talked as they were walking and wrote nothing.

What did they talk about? Best to ask the Critic who, as usual, was hanging about them. However, the Critic was not eager to tell anyone what he had heard, except, perhaps, the Secretary at Party House, but the Secretary did not receive him today. The Secretary had something more important to do: he was reading a report Jozef had written about the Bearded Poet.

And that night Jozef dreamed that he was walking along some tracks between the rails when suddenly he saw a train speeding straight at him. It was a terrible dream. He tried to get off the tracks, but could not move his legs; it was as if someone had poured lead into them. Then, Jozek from one side, and the Critic from the other, began tugging Jozef, one by his right hand, and one by his left, but he could not be budged. And now the engine was close... closer... and hot steam scalded his face.

He woke up dazed with fear. When he came to himself, he jumped out of bed, lit the night-light and wrote down his dream, because by morning he would certainly have forgotten it. Then he lit a cigarette, sat for a while, and lay down again. Content with himself, he slept long and well. But when he woke up and read what he had written during the night, he got angry and tore his writing into little pieces, and thought, 'things are bad with me, very bad. I've lost my gift and I am writing like a hack. A bit more and I'll be better at reading dreams or telling fortunes with cards than writing.' He went to the milk-bar to have his breakfast. 'To be a writer,' he thought again, 'I stayed a bachelor, but...'

'Good morning, Comrade Secretary,' someone said to Jozef, someone he didn't know at all.

'Ah, that's it,' he thought. 'It's because I'm the Secretary that first I dream rubbish, then I write rubbish, all the time thinking that I am an artist.' And he became very sad, so sad that he did not finish his coffee or his beloved soft-boiled egg.

Chapter 4
THE NEW CHAIRMAN

'I'm already tired of writing about this,' said Jozek.

'Writing our story bores you?' Jozef was surprised.

'No, but I've had enough of your Secretaries, all their yakking, and that Critic. You're so taken up with them that you've completely forgotten about our yard,' Jozek explained.

'I understand and agree with you but, believe me, there's no other way. You don't want me to stop writing about myself, do you?... And, well, I too am a Secretary, and well...'

'Well, nobody made you be one, did they?' Jozek interrupted him. 'Don't be one and that's that.'

'It's not quite as simple as it seems,' and Jozef thought for a while, lit a cigarette, and became sad again.

Jozek felt sorry for big Jozef and said, 'All right, let's write about it, but just this once, not any more.'

'And that's why, Comrade Potoczek,' said the Secretary at Party House, 'we have to organize a Congress of the Writers' Union. You prepare your speech for the Congress in accordance with the directives from Party House and bring it to us for approval. Also prepare a few comrades for the discussion, let's say about a dozen. It would be good if the Bearded Poet would talk about the function of poetry. You've known each other long enough... I know, I know what you want to tell me. I have read your report about his dropping out from the Party, but that's nothing – don't worry about it. A poet doesn't have to be a Party member; it's even better if he isn't. We have considered all this and have come to the conclusion that the Bearded Poet is today the best candidate for the New Chairman. Don't be surprised, Comrade Potoczek. You've read the latest news in the Western press. Our enemies have made a national hero out of the Bearded Poet because he flung down his Party membership card, and they predict he will be expelled from the Writers' Union any day now and perhaps even locked up. These Western scandal-lovers and – let us be frank – provocation-lovers, have even prepared protests and started to collect signatures under an appeal for the release of the Bearded Poet from prison, while we... we will make him Chairman of the Writers' Union. Ah, I see you like this game. But it is not a game; it is a struggle with the enemy from whom we must wrest a weapon. Of course, the election of the Bearded Poet as the Chairman of our Writers' Union will immediately be understood as a rebellion of the whole Union against our Party. Interest in our literature will immediately quicken in the West, they will translate and publish our books, but we'll see to it that everything goes our way. And so to work, Comrade Potoczek.'

'Best we take a taxi,' said Jozek. 'It's Sunday, the Bearded Poet lives a long way away and we might not find him at home. On days like this he might go fishing.'

A little girl opened the door for them. Jozef went in first, then Jozek who straight away tried to pull her pigtail. She stuck her tongue out at him and led the way down a hallway. She stopped at a door, opened it quietly, peeped inside, then closed it quietly and whispered, 'Please wait. Mr. Poet is writing poems now and can't be interrupted, because his inspiration might leave him.'

They did not wait long. The Poet said, 'Come in!' and they went into the room with the little girl behind them. The Bearded Poet was sitting in an armchair with his legs propped up on a little table, smoking a pipe.

'What a surprise!' he called out. 'The Party Mountain has come to Mohammed. Sit down, friend, here, on the settee. It's quite comfortable, and you love comfort. Sit down and tell me what you've come about and what on earth brings you here. And you, Haneczka, look after the Comrade Writer's assistant. What's your name, you hooligan?' and he winked at him.

'Jozek.'

Jozek took a liking to the Bearded Poet so forgave him the 'hooligan' and winked back. Only Haneczka remained serious, as befits a mistress of the house. She took Jozek by the hand and led him into the next room.

'Help me dust the books,' she said and gave Jozek a cloth. She set to work as well. 'That's my brother. He writes poems. And that man must be your father.'

'And so to work, Comrade Potoczek' (page 38)

'No,' muttered Jozek, 'he's my friend, and we're writing a story together,' said Jozek and twitched her pigtail.

'Don't be cheeky with me,' but she did not stick out her tongue.

She stood on a chair and started to dust the shelves, and Jozek took the books she handed down to him.

'Why has that man come to see my brother?' she asked.

'To talk to him,' answered Jozek.

'Does he write books for children?'

'He writes for children, and I write for grown-ups — not for you.'

'Of course not for me. I'm lucky I'm not your teacher and don't have to read your schoolboy compositions.'

From the next room, where Jozef was talking with the Poet, they could hear the sounds of a quarrel. They went to the door and listened.

'Was your brother in the Underground during the Occupation?'

'Yes,' Haneczka replied, 'what about your friend?'

'Uh huh,' said Jozek.

'And did he take part in the Uprising?'

'He did.'

'Then maybe they were in the same unit and got to know each other there.'

'Maybe, but my friend was in a Peoples' one.'

'And my brother was in a National one and afterwards he had to go to jail for it. Someone informed on him and reported that he was concealing weapons, but it wasn't true. They wanted my brother to confess he'd spied for the enemy, but he didn't confess and they tortured him a lot. He couldn't stand it any longer and slit his throat. Now he wears a beard so you can't see the scar. Then they freed him, publicly cleared him, signed him into the Party...'

'And then?'

'Now he's broken with them.'

'With whom?' asked Jozef.

'You ask me as if you didn't know. The Jews!' shouted the Bearded Poet. 'They taught me this hatred, tortured me, stamped on me, humiliated me, and taught me! What is more, they still rule us! And you're telling fairy tales about how things have changed.'

'Listen,' Jozef put in, 'just tell me this. Would you, two years or even one year ago, have dared to fling down your Party membership card? Or would I, the Party Secretary, have come to a man who flung down his card in my presence, a man blinded by the wrong done him (though you've since been rehabilitated) and tried to talk that man into becoming Chairman of the Union? – And not on my own initiative, either. Whether in the Party or outside it, every decent man in a top post has the obligation to contribute gradually and steadily to the intensification of present change, both through his work and through his influence on others, so as to prevent any attempt to return to the recent past. Who is to be this man for us? Who is to be this for us in the Party, in literature, in administration; in a word, wherever we are?'

Haneczka opened the door and ran up to the Bearded Poet, who was sitting in the armchair digging at his pipe. She leaned over him and started whispering in his ear, 'Say yes, please, please, say yes; I do so want you to be a Chairman.'

The Bearded Poet laughed and said, 'All right, we'll see, you little weasel,' and gave her a pat. Haneczka ran back to Jozek who was standing in the doorway and they went off to dust the books.

And that night Jozef saw how the Poet's friends from

his unit came to him, and how the Poet ordered them to enter the Party and all the cultural organizations, so that after they were in control... What they were meant to do when they were in control, the Bearded Poet had no chance to say, for the telephone rang. Jozef rose, picked up the receiver, but it turned out to be a wrong number.

Chapter 5
INSPIRATION

Jozef, as we know, is a writer. But many different people are considered writers — for instance, all those who belong to the Writers' Union. Jozef, it is true, belongs to the Union, but that is not why he is a writer. Why then? Because he has talent. It happens, however, that talent is not enough. Inspiration is also necessary, but it can never be summoned by a writer, even when he is a member of the Union — it comes or goes according to its own whim, controlled by nothing and no one. Inspiration does not like noise, does not like witnesses, sometimes does not even like the light of day.

Jozef knew this very well. And so he would ask the Not Unattractive Secretary to take his calls. All those that had any business with 'The Comrade Secretary' were to be told he was busy. He would lock himself in his office, draw the curtains, even turn on a small table lamp, but inspiration would not come. Then Jozef would leave the office, take a tram back to his one-room flat with its two gas burners in the kitchenette just next to the bathroom, make himself some strong Turkish coffee and wait again for inspiration. Sometimes it came, sometimes it did not, recently less and less often. And indeed, it happened once that inspiration did come but Jozef was unable to write even a single sentence.

For Jozef was not a typical writer. Apart from talent and inspiration, he had to have little Jozek at his side to write. Then why would he never invite Jozek to his tiny flat? Obviously not because the alarm clock on his bed-side table was not broken. One could break the alarm clock or even do away with it, but one could not break, let alone do away with the clock ticking intrusively behind the wall in the flat next door. In that flat someone snored at night and pottered about constantly during the day, someone who was not a member of the Union and did not have to listen to Jozef.

So Jozef would quit his small room, take a tram again, and go to the grey tenement where Jozek played in the yard. And this is what he did now.

He came in through the front entry, bowed to Rachel who was rushing off to the shops, and passed into the yard but did not find Jozek. He remembered then that actually it was morning and Jozek was certainly at school. Unfortunately, Jozek was not there either. And little Goldberg thought a bit and said, 'Maybe he's sick. Maybe he's got a sore throat.' Jozef went back to the grey tenement. On the way he visited Satan and the café on the corner, but there was still no sign of Jozek. He got into the flat because Rachel, who had forgotten to buy salt, had run back out to the shops; he opened the door to the second room, where there were two beds side by side covered with one red-flowered bedspread and under the window an ottoman covered with a bedspread too, only yellow-flowered — again there was no Jozek. What could he do? Rachel came back and Jozef tried to hide, but he did not need to because Rachel went back to the shop once again, having forgotten to buy matches.

'Where can he be?' Jozef asked himself.

He asked a little too loudly, for he awakened the hedgehog sleeping in the corner under the coat rack. The annoyed hedgehog stamped its feet, and Jozef took alarm and ran off.

Suddenly, when he was back in the street, inspiration came to him. He sat on the steps leading to a green stand labelled 'Health Food' that sold beer as well, and began to write. He did not write for long because he was interrupted by the Critic.

'Good morning, my dear colleague,' he said and sat down next to Jozef.

Jozef put his hand over the sheet he had been writing on. He did not want the Critic to see that he was writing about the yard again. Very angry that the Critic had interrupted him, he asked, 'And what are you doing here?'

'I have a free day today,' answered the Critic, who was not put off by such a reception, 'and I am taking advantage of it to do some reading.'

He took the latest issue of the 'Literary Gazette' out of his pocket, spread it out on his knees, and started reading an article Jozef had written about the Party as a source of literary inspiration.

Jozef was a little ashamed that he had been so unpleasant to the Critic. He wanted to apologize, but instead he asked him, 'Do you know where little Jozek could be?'

'I do,' said the Critic. 'He's run away from home.'

Jozef was not surprised but rather saddened only and, paying no more attention to the Critic, started to write again. He wrote about why little Jozek had run away from home.

'Jozek ran away from home,' big Jozef began, 'because although he loved his parents very much, he could not forgive them for bringing him up to be a Jew.'

'What rubbish!' Jozek would have said if he had read it. 'Just a pile of rubbish!' First of all, Jozek had certainly never thought about whether he loved his parents or not. Parents are simply things one has. And only when one is grown-up and does not have them any more does one love them. Secondly, Jozek did not know what his parents were bringing him up to be. They were always talking about trying to bring him up to be a decent upright person, but what did that mean? One could perhaps accept that every decent upright person should learn to read, write and count, and that to learn these things he should go to school. And Jozek did go to school. He had even started going to religion, although he did not like it when the teacher kissed him. But why did his Papa take on that rabbi who comes twice a week to teach Jozek to mark down squiggles in Hebrew which, to make things more difficult, have to be written from the right to the left. That rabbi always stinks so badly that, although Jozek sits on the other side of the table, he still has to turn away and cannot look at the book. And why does that rabbi, who always wears his skull-cap, make Jozek wear a cap during lessons?

And thirdly, Jozek did not run away from home at all. For where could he run away to! Not to Goldberg,

Inspiration does not like noise, does not like witnesses,
sometimes does not even like the light of day (page 43)

for everything would immediately be found out. To Staszek? No again. True, Jozek had thought of going off into the world, but he immediately felt sorry for himself wandering about the streets, hungry, cold, shivering in the rain. And what could he do in the winter? He would freeze to death somewhere, like that Little Match Girl. But if he were to sell his penknife and his books? And his mother's red beads and his father's pocket watch? He could carefully take it from the drawer of his father's bedside table while his father was asleep. He would also take a whole loaf of bread, put all these things in his satchel, and run away into the night. Only the entry is locked at night. Or maybe he could do it another way. Go off in the morning as if he were going to school and then run away. Mama would be waiting for him with lunch, but he would not come back. It would be evening now, Papa would come home from work, and he still would not be there. They would look for him, ask the other boys in the yard, first Staszek, then Heniek, then go to his school and find that he had not been there, and go to the police. Mama would be crying... and Jozek felt sorry for his mother. The police would obviously find him and bring him back home, and then everyone would find out that he had run away from home and was not afraid to go out into the world like a grown-up.

But what if they only found him after a week? Where would he sleep? Maybe it would be better not to run away for long. For a few days. Even one day would be enough. And hide so that Mama would find him herself. In the wardrobe? No, that would not be running away. In the cellar? The attic would be best. Through the little window he would be able to see what was going on in the yard — the way his mother would be looking for him, talking to children and neighbours.

No doubt big Jozef must have forgotten all this when he grew up. And, although he had inspiration, he wrote some more rubbish.

'Little Jozek,' wrote big Jozef, 'had a great sense of justice, and by running away from home he protested against dividing people according to their ethnic origin, although this protest was as yet an unconscious one.'

But actually the truth was this:

Jozek would hide from the rabbi so that his mother couldn't find him, the rabbi would wait an hour, drink tea, talk with his mother, and go away. But Papa heard about this, had a fit and, had it not been for Mama, might have given Jozek a thrashing. Jozek could even have stood the thrashing, but Papa had said, 'If you don't like our home, you little Goy, then go and find another, go find some other parents. Nobody will cry for you here; you can go wherever you like!' This Jozek could not forgive — everything else, yes, but that they should throw him out of his home, no. We shall see if they don't go looking for him, calling after him. And his Mama would surely cry, and so would his Papa. Didn't he cry, didn't he call out in anguish when Jozek had been choking, sick with diphtheria? He must have forgotten that by now.

Big Jozef, a grown-up like Papa, had not remembered much either since he wrote:

'Little Jozek had chosen the railway station for his escape. And, due to human indifference, no one concerned himself with why a little boy with a school satchel was wandering around the busy and dangerous streets of the city at a time when all other children were at school.'

And little Jozek was sitting safely in the attic. He sat by a small window and looked down into the yard. He saw his mother return from the shops. 'How small Mama is from here,' he thought. 'I'm bigger than she is.' The yard was empty. Jozek decided he was hungry. He took a roll out of his satchel, but it had cheese in it. He put it aside. He began to wander around the attic and got entangled in a sheet drying on the line, went back to his window, took out his exercise book, ripped out a few pages, and began to make paper planes. When the boys came home from school, he could fly his paper planes to give a clue where to look for him. Szymonowa pushed a cart with some buckets on it into the yard. Jozek stuck his head out of the window and spat, but he missed. He threw down a few pieces of brick, hit a bucket and Szymonowa in the back just as she was bending over. He saw her look around and shake her fist, but not in his direction. He liked this a lot so he did it again. This time he threw down a whole handful of brick chippings, which scattered over the whole yard. Szymonowa cursed and ran inside. After a moment he heard her coming up the stairs towards the attic. He hid behind a post but she spied him, grabbed his collar, and marched to his Mama, who was standing on the balcony.

Meanwhile, big Jozef wrote how little Jozek was found in another city, after stowing away on a train.

Jozef had no time to write what happened next, for he heard the Critic who had been sitting quietly next to him all the time start snoring over his paper. Because of that snoring, inspiration left Jozef and he could not write any more. He got up, put the written sheets into his pocket, and went up the steps to the Health Food stand. He asked for a coffee but they only had one made from grain and had run out of milk. He drank some beer and went back to the grey tenement to see what had been going on. He was coming out onto the first floor landing when he saw Szymonowa holding Jozek by the collar and marching him to Rachel. Big

Jozef was very ashamed, even wanted to apologize to Szymonowa, but he had to go to the Union, as it was nearly time for lunch.

And the Critic went on snoring and dreamed that the police had caught Jozek and that, for travelling on a train without a ticket, he was sent to a special school for problem children where he, the Critic, was now the instructor.

Chapter 6
MARYLA

Maryla painted her fingernails violet, wore a very short and tight skirt, drank coffee in the Union cafeteria, and was writing an anti-novel. Jozef found her rather attractive, but she annoyed little Jozek because her hair was always a mess. The Bearded Poet called her Anti-Maryla and thought that she could have been worse looking but wasn't exactly his idea of a bed-mate. The Critic saw things differently: he believed in young literati and, when he did not have to write reports, treated Maryla to a coffee.

'My dear colleague,' he said to Jozef, 'we should arrange a six-month grant for her, and take more interest in her work.'

Maryla brought Jozef seven written sheets of paper to read, said that this was the first anti-chapter, said that she would write a second as soon as she had some anti-inspiration, and asked when she could get a little cash. Jozef corrected her and said 'anti-cash', but Maryla declared that this was impossible as the building of Socialism had not yet been completed, and so anti-stockings and anti-dinners were not yet provided for constitutionally. The Critic laughed and said that she was only making an innocent joke and that there was no need to mention it in his report to Party House. He took Maryla by the hand and they went off together, and Jozef started to read the first chapter. He read it three times very carefully, but still could not understand why Zeus betrayed Hera with Lumumba who had eaten Tschombe's mistress for breakfast. Nevertheless, he got Maryla her grant.

Maryla did not take Jozek seriously, calling him an infant and his yard a bourgeois tomb. Only Rachel appealed to her, because Rachel had run away from home. Maryla did not believe in love, and she spent the night at Jozef's simply because he had a roof over his head and hot running water in his bathroom. In his shoes, she said, she would have gone to the Writers' Congress in Rome and chosen freedom.

She slept until noon, so Jozef had to leave her by herself in his room, because he was going to the Union. On his way he bought a morning paper and read... no, the newspapers did not write about an actual arrest because they did not want to write too hastily since matters had not been clarified. So Jozef learned of the arrest of the writer Maczka at the news-stand.

'Good morning, Mr. Secretary,' the newsagent greeted Jozef. 'You know, don't you, sir, that he's been locked up?'

'Who?' asked Jozef.

'That Maczka of course.'

'They've arrested the writer Maczka?' Jozef was astonished, but rallied immediately, as it would not befit him to appear ignorant of such a thing, and corrected himself at once. 'Oh yes... that's right.'

'Serves him right,' continued the newsagent, who also sold toilet soaps from his stand. 'Probably not satisfied with all the honours and medals he's got, and wanted dollars as well.'

'Dollars?' Jozef was again surprised.

'Of course dollars. We know about these things. Maczka probably had at least a dozen women on the string and was still slandering our youth in that Paris gutter rag. Maybe he thought that nobody would catch on if he used a pseudonym. And for this kind of slur on the reputation of our youth dollars are sprinkled very generously.'

'But how do you know about that?'

'What? You don't think I can read newspapers?' The vendor was offended. 'Here, just read that, Mr. Secretary.'

And Jozef read 'Hostile Invectives' — that was the headline, and beneath, in the tenth line, standing out in bold type: 'Our society indignantly condemns the underhanded work of certain writers who, in search of sensation and cheap publicity, publish slanderous articles in the Western press which are the products of a diseased imagination and criminal delusions about our new generation of youth...' He read on — the parts which were not made to stand out as well — but found no mention of Maczka.

'They haven't actually mentioned that Maczka yet,'

explained the vendor, 'but they will. The court will give him a good few years, and then they'll mention him.'

'Well, that's it,' thought Jozef. 'I don't keep up with things. I probably write too much and read too little, and besides, there's Jozek and that Maryla.'

'I've just seen Maryla,' said the Bearded Poet. 'She thinks, and I know you care about her opinion, that you should take a vacation to catch up on your reading because you don't keep up with the times.'

'She said that too?'

'What do you mean "too"?'

'Oh nothing, just something I said,' Jozef blurted out, and ran off to the grey tenement. I must fix that infernal clock, he said to himself. I can't stand this any longer.

He went up to the first floor, noticed with slight surprise that on the Mazurkiewicz's door there was someone else's name-plate, then stepped up his pace, opened the door of Jozek's flat, and stood transfixed. On the kitchen wall the clock that had been broken was now ticking!

'Who do you want?' The man who came out of the other room was wearing his shirt unbuttoned and holding a pair of pliers.

'I-I'am sorry,' stammered Jozef. 'I thought... sorry, it's a mistake.'

'Who are you anyway?'

'Me? well... an acquaintance.'

'Whose acquaintance? Surely not mine?'

'No, not yours... of the Hirszfelds.'

'Hirszfelds? What Hirszfelds?'

'They used to live here...'

'Oh I see, I get it now. When they were moved into the ghetto I exchanged flats with them. Still, that was a long time ago. And you say you're a friend of theirs?'

'Well, sort of.'

'So you're a foreigner, maybe?'

'A foreigner? Why?'

'One of us wouldn't be looking for the Hirszfelds after so many years. Everyone here knows that they're all dead now, and those who did make it have different names and wouldn't live in a dump like this. You'd be looking for them in the quarter where the high-ups live, not here.'

He went up to the clock and began to adjust it with his pliers. And while his back was turned, Jozef left quickly.

He walked along the street, passed the green Health Food stand and then the corner café which now also sold beer. He stood at the tram stop and saw little Jozek running to school but Jozek did not recognize him. Jozef ran after Jozek, suddenly tripped and fell, hurting his elbow badly, and began to sob out loud.

'Quiet, please, stop it,' a terrified Maryla begged him, 'for God's sake, stop it' and she pulled Jozef's hair, but he wouldn't wake up.

Chapter 7
THE STOLEN BIOGRAPHY

'First Heniek stuck his tongue out at me,' said a tear-ful Jozek, 'then he shook his fist at me and told me that today my last hour had come. He always says that...'

Jozef took another chocolate out of his pocket, re-moved the silver paper, and popped it into Jozek's mouth.

'And what happened next?' asked the Critic.

'I went for a break because the bell had just rung, but I kept close to my teacher so that Heniek couldn't do anything to me. The teacher was walking along the corridor and I followed her. Then she went into the staff room, and I tried to hide in the lavatory, but

Heniek saw me and jumped at me from behind, twisted my arm and gave me a full nelson. "I've got you at last, you stinking creep. I'm not going to let go! You just wait, I'm not going to let you go!" I pleaded, promised him my catapult and anything else he wanted, but he kept on saying, "I'm not going to let you go, not until you return my biography, you thief!" '

'He said "my biography?" asked Jozef. 'Did he really say that?'

'Yes, just like that, "my biography", and I didn't understand what he meant. I didn't get him at first and thought he was joking. He's always making fun of me and pinching me. Once he told our teacher I'd stolen his composition, but I hadn't — he copied it from me. The teacher believed him and I got a zero.'

'You can tell us about the composition afterwards,' said the Critic impatiently. 'Tell us now about the biography.'

'He said I'd stolen his biography and without a biography he couldn't be in the Party.'

'You're making something up,' said the Critic. 'He could not possibly have said that.'

'He could,' Jozef put in, 'he could, and he probably did.'

'You're talking poppycock, my dear colleague. Although...' and the Critic became very gloomy.

'Unfortunately,' said Jozef, 'it is quite possible that the clock belonging to Major Mazurkiewicz has been broken, too, and stopped or suddenly started going backwards. It is quite likely. Just remember what the Secretary at Party House said. The Comrade Secretary said we must make up time — make up for lost time, that is — and time lost is time held back by someone. The Comrade Secretary did not mention any names, but I'm sure he meant Major Mazurkiewicz and his...

well, you understand, my friend, what's in my mind, don't you?'

'Yes,' the Critic confirmed, 'but you cannot write about Major Mazurkiewicz's clock-fiddling in your report to Party House because you have been doing the same thing... and I warned you, I reasoned with you, I pleaded with you, dear colleague, and yet you carried on, and now you made your bed, you must lie on it.'

Jozef was silent and didn't raise his bowed head. He was very distressed because he realized it was all his fault. And little Jozek was washing down his chocolate with soda water, and would have calmed down completely if the Critic hadn't started pestering him again for details.

'All right then,' he asked, 'but this Mazurkiewicz... well, this Heniek, how did he find the manuscript?'

'It was with Satan,' answered Jozek.

'With Satan!' The Critic and Jozef exclaimed together in astonishment. 'Why did Satan let him into his kennel?'

'Because Satan made a mistake. He thought that Heniek was me.'

'The blind, stupid old animal,' said the Critic angrily.

He said this because he was unjust, unjust to the ever honest and ever faithful Satan. It happens that grown-ups — and not only grown-ups but children as well — tell lies and believe them. This is particularly true of writers, who, so as not to be suspected of lying, call their lies fiction and become quite proud of them, and even get awards from people who think that fiction is truth. With dogs it is different. Take Satan for example. Satan was not blind at all, nor had he made a mistake. He is honest and never tells lies, and has never been interested in fiction, that is, in lies. And anyway, how was he to know that Jozef had made Heniek into Jozek and that Jozek had appropriated facts from Heniek's biography? How could a simple creature know that this

59

was all fiction and, what is more, creative fiction for which writers sometimes receive awards. Satan does not understand these things. He is a dog, not a writer — nor even a reader since he is not interested in the affairs of others. Satan thought that Heniek was the real Jozek, and let him into his kennel.

So it happened. Now big Henryk would find out everything from little Heniek, and would write a report on Jozef to the Secretary at Party House. If Henryk Mazurkiewicz were a writer, like Jozef Potoczek, then all this would not be so terrible. At worst he would accuse his colleague of plagiarism or of stealing his theme. Such things happen and the Secretary at Party House is not the least bit interested in them. But Henryk Mazurkiewicz is the Major and responsible for Security, which is to say, he ferrets out people who want to conceal something from the Comrade Secretary.

'I warned you, my dear colleague,' the Critic spoke again, 'that you should not have concealed anything. You should have listened to me about that questionnaire and not delved into those racist reflections on peeing. And with your entreaties you got my silence as well. Now I am your accomplice.'

'But perhaps Mazurkiewicz will decide to forget the whole affair, and won't go ahead with it,' said Jozef. 'After all, he too has been tampering with time.'

'I doubt he will,' said the Critic. 'He could have done it deliberately, just to catch you out. He knows what he's doing.'

'So you think,' continued Jozef, 'that when the Comrade Secretary said we must make up for lost time, he was not thinking of the Major, but...'

'That's right. Not of him, but of you. And possibly the Comrade Secretary already knows,' concluded the Critic.

'What to do? What to do?' said Jozef, clutching his head again.

And little Jozek really began to cry.

And so the three of them sat together on the steps leading up to the green stand labelled 'Health Food'. The shop assistant saw them through the window and was not the least bit moved by Jozek's blubbering. Maybe she was insensitive or just so bored that nothing really mattered to her any more. Probably bored, since she yawned openly and from time to time she applied fresh lipstick to her lips. There were no customers today as she had run out of both coffee made of grain and beer. Instead there was only soda water, warm, that's true, but no matter as the day was not very hot.

Opposite the food stand, in the doorway of the grocery store, stood another bored shop assistant, who had just weighed out half a kilo of salt for Rachel.

Rachel was walking home, wondering what she should make for dinner. The cauliflower fell out of her bag, she turned to pick it up and saw Jozek. She ran up to him, and took no notice of big Jozef. Seeing her son crying she would certainly not have noticed the Critic either, but there was no need to for, as soon as he noticed her, he went away.

'Jozek, my baby, what's wrong? Why didn't you come home? Are you ill? Tell Mama where it hurts you.' And she placed her hand on his forehead to see if he had a temperature.

Jozek glanced secretly at Jozef because he didn't know what he should say if she asked him why he was crying. For the moment he simply said, 'my tummy's hurting a little bit and I think I'm going to be sick.' But actually he said this because he had seen the cauliflower.

'Come on then,' said his mother, 'I'll put you to bed and take your temperature. God help us, it might be dysentery. Oh Lord, that I should mention such a name!'

Then Jozef rose, doffed his hat, bowed gallantly and said courteously, 'Please forgive me, Madam, but by chance I witnessed a very unpleasant scene at your son's school. Heniek Mazurkiewicz beat up Jozek and insulted him with some uncensored epithets.'

Rachel was somewhat taken aback by the words of this elegant gentleman and did not understand the phrase 'uncensored epithets', but though she was a simple woman, she immediately grasped everything.

'Oh my God,' she exclaimed, 'when will that Goy brat leave my child alone?' And to Jozek, 'How many times have I told you to keep away from him, to go three miles out of your way to avoid him. You never listen to me, and now look. I've pleaded with you so hard! He will make you a cripple. My God, oh my God, what times these are, why do you punish me so!'

Jozek was silent, but big Jozef continued, 'You should do something right now. The thuggery of young Mazurkiewicz should be punished in an exemplary fashion and...'

As he was saying this he noticed the terrified look on Jozek's face and remembered the biography and stopped. He wanted to say good-bye to Rachel and hurry off to the Union to ask the Not Unattractive Secretary if, by any chance, there had been a call from Major Mazurkiewicz. But he could not move. He felt very sorry for Rachel, who was sad and spread her arms out helplessly.

'You are so unusual,' she said timidly. 'You say "should be punished", but who is going to listen to me, a simple Jewish woman? Such is my fate...'

And Jozef saw her tears. He felt even sorrier for Rachel and said, 'I will help you, Madam. I myself will speak to those Mazurkiewiczes.' He said this and immediately felt a little angry at himself for having said it, but it was too late.

Rachel lifted her head and looked at him hopefully, murmuring, 'Thank you, sir, thank you.'

They all three went together to the grey tenement, Rachel on one side, Jozef on the other, and little Jozek in the middle.

When they reached the Mazurkiewiczes' door, Rachel suddenly hesitated, 'perhaps you would like to visit us first?'

Jozef agreed with alacrity. Rachel opened the door and, in embarrassment, apologized to Jozef that the kitchen is untidy, she can't invite him into the other room, because the beds aren't made, the washerwoman is coming today and there is no sense in cleaning up because, you know yourself, sir, what washing means, real Gomorrah.

Rachel asked Jozef to be seated in a chair she wiped over with her apron, asked him if he would like some tea, and said that, all in all, it would be better if Jakub and not she were to go to the Mazurkiewiczes. But Jozef did not have time and thanked her all the same for the tea, so Rachel went into the other room sighing heavily, to change a bit and comb her hair.

Only then did Jozek ask quietly, 'and the biography?'

Jozef thought and replied, 'best not to tell anyone about it. I'll try to sort things out somehow.'

He said this to calm Jozek down, but in fact he had no idea what to do. He even thought that, if Rachel kept on hesitating about the visit to the Mazurkiewiczes, then he would not insist.

Rachel returned in a new dress and told Jozek to go to bed immediately and take his temperature.

Big Jozef had a feeling she was eyeing him rather strangely. After a moment she said, 'I'm very sorry about that ugly word. I hope you weren't offended with me, sir?'

'What word?' said Jozef in surprise.

Rachel blushed and whispered, 'I said, and I beg your pardon, sir, I called Heniek "a Goy brat". You are not Jewish yourself, but you were not offended by an unfortunate mother, were you, sir?'

Jozef laughed, 'and how do you know that I'm not a Jew? Perhaps I am.'

Rachel was very confused, but she stopped looking at him strangely, and said almost gaily, 'If you are a Jew, sir, then you will understand me, you really will know what it means to live in a Goy block. How many tears have I shed over my Jozek! Poor child. You couldn't even imagine what that scamp did to him when he was barely eight years old. Along with some other young ruffians, Heniek pulled down my Jozek's trousers and...'

Rachel became flustered once more and did not look at Jozef. To little Jozek she said, 'Go into the other room and lie down, son. I'll have a chat with this gentleman.'

When Jozek had gone, Rachel changed to Yiddish, and Jozef had to pretend that he understood everything, though in truth he understood nothing at all. But he did not have to because he knew the whole story anyway. He just nodded his head, and Rachel complained. She did not even spare Jakub, who does not want to move to a tenement where Jews live. She keeps begging him, and he always says, 'Don't be silly. Where else than among Goys will I find so many lawyers, chairmen and directors who will give me tips for a simple "Your Honour", "I am at your service, your Excellency". Who is going to come to me for a haircut every week and a shave every day, Jews maybe?' He works in a Goy district and must live in a Goy district so he can be near his work and come home for a meal during the day. Does she, Rachel, want to go to the other end of town to bring him his meal in a pot, and is he to eat it warmed over? Isn't it better that he works and earns their keep, and she, Rachel, just looks after their home and watches over their son? And Rachel watches over him as much as she can. She even takes him to school and picks him up, not every day, true, but then Jozek is now in the fourth grade... And anyway how can she make sure he does nothing wrong? Obviously she cannot sit with him at school.

And Rachel started to complain about Jozek, that he disobeys, that he runs away from the rabbi, that, although she forbids him to play in the yard — isn't the balcony enough for him — he still goes around with those rascals who would beat a Jewish child to death. Thank God that Jozek is doing well at school and likes reading. At least he has something to keep him busy, for she, Rachel, cannot always go for a walk with him. She knows that the child needs fresh air, and this year she will make Jakub let her take Jozek to the mountains for his vacation, but then, who would stay with Jakub?

Jozef listened, nodded his head, and was even happy that Rachel had forgotten they were to go to the Mazurkiewiczes.

But Rachel had not forgotten at all.

'Well, we can go now,' she said, and stood aside to let Jozef go first.

'It really is impossible what these naughty children get up to,' Mrs. Mazurkiewicz was saying, as she rolled out some dough for noodles, or perhaps for dumplings, because it was getting late and Mr. Mazurkiewicz was coming home for his meal. 'But such words?... Where could Henryk have learned them? Certainly not at home. Our family,' continued Mrs. Mazurkiewicz with great feeling, 'is well-known for its spirit of tolerance and humanity...'

Jozef was standing by the table listening and Rachel stood behind him close to the door, also listening. There were, to be sure, four chairs and two stools, but Mrs. Mazurkiewicz had not asked them to sit down.

'... and our son Henryk has been brought up in the best patriotic tradition. We welcome Israelites in our home,' here Mrs. Mazurkiewicz looked at Rachel, 'like the Baruchs, and Mr. Wilhelm Kugelman, the parliamentary candidate, sends season's greetings every year to Mr. Mazurkiewicz. We have been neighbours of the Hirszfelds for several years and you must admit,' and she looked again at Rachel, 'that there have never been any conflicts between us. But boys will be boys, and in these times,' here she looked at Jozef, 'ever since our Marshal died, everything has been turned upside-down. The riff-raff are everywhere and poison the minds of our children. It must have been that Antek, the son of that shoemaker in the basement, who taught Henryk such words. To think that cultured people have to live in the same building with such riff-raff.'

Mrs. Mazurkiewicz sprinkled the dough with flour, covered it with a white napkin, and Jozef, who had no desire to meet Mr. Mazurkiewicz and Heniek, decided that his mission was over. He wanted to say something polite in leaving, but instead he said, 'Please excuse me, I forgot to introduce myself. My name is Potoczek, Jozef Potoczek.'

When he said this, something unexpected happened. Mrs. Mazurkiewicz whisked off her apron and exclaimed, 'Oh dear, I beg your pardon. Do forgive me!' She ran to the sink and started to wash the flour off her hands, exclaiming all the while, 'I should have recognized you at once! I have seen your photograph so many times!

66

What a great honour for our house! The famous writer Jozef Potoczek has crossed our doorstep. What an honour indeed!'

She ran up to Jozef, held out her hand, which Jozef kissed, and again starts to apologize, asks him to take a seat, if only for a moment. She doesn't dare to invite him into the other room because the floor has not been polished. Housekeeping takes up so much time, not to mention bringing up a son. 'Only by going without sleep could we keep up with the latest developments in contemporary culture and art. Only in the evenings can we listen to Chopin and read our great writers. And we have not been in a café for at least a month... your latest book...'

Here Mrs. Mazurkiewicz hurried off into the other room and, forgetting that the floor had not yet been polished, left the door wide open. From his large portrait, which hung between the two windows, the Marshal looked down at Jozef. He was obviously displeased, for he was frowning with his bushy eyebrows. Below him hung the somewhat smaller portrait of the National Bard.

Mrs. Mazurkiewicz brought out a copy of Jozef's book, and asked him to be so kind as to autograph the title page. Mr. Mazurkiewicz would never have forgiven his wife, were their private library denied such an honour. Jozef signed, and Mrs. Mazurkiewicz asked him if he would come to a dinner party on Thursday, to which she was also inviting...

Jozef was no longer listening. He was even beginning to be impatient, but Mrs. Mazurkiewicz did not stop talking.

Rachel was becoming impatient as well, because Jakub was about to come home for his meal and she had not even had time to light the fire in the stove, which is why she muttered something.

Jozef seized the moment to say, 'This is very kind of you, Madam, but I'm not sure if my responsibilities will permit me. I will let you know,' he was going to say 'through Jozek' but he checked himself and said 'through Mrs. Hirszfeld.'

'My dear lady, my good neighbour!' Mrs. Mazurkiewicz exclaimed and came up to Rachel, 'only you must not forget, we would be extremely grateful...'

She was still speaking when Jozef, having kissed the hand of a flustered Rachel, was hurrying downstairs. At the entry he nearly ran into Heniek, who brushed against him. It seemed to Jozef that Heniek had managed to pinch him in the thigh.

And that night he dreamed that the Secretary at Party House had summoned Major Mazurkiewicz and yelled at him... And Jozef would certainly have learned what the Comrade Secretary was so angry about, had not the alarm clock gone off.

Chapter 8
THE MANUSCRIPT RETURNED

Any sensible person whose manuscript had been taken by Major Mazurkiewicz would certainly have stopped writing and begun to consider the best way to escape trouble. Then why did Jozef go on writing? Why had he written the seventh chapter and was now writing the eighth? Because a writer does not have to be sensible.

There was another reason, too. On the same day that this misfortune occurred, Heniek came to Jozek in the evening and returned the manuscript. 'I'll give the scribble back to you,' he said, 'and I'll even forgive you for stealing my biography, but for that you give me your catapult, your hedgehog, and your pocket knife, because mine is broken.'

Jozek agreed immediately, gave Heniek his catapult, his hedgehog, and his pocket knife, and was so happy that he could not sleep all night and kept the manuscript under the pillow, and the next morning, instead of going to school, he ran off to see Jozef. He had never been to Jozef's, but knew where he lived.

Big Jozef was making tea and sandwiches for himself and for Maryla who was still lying in bed. When he saw a breathless but radiant Jozek he was so amazed that he almost forgot to turn off the alarm clock on the bedside table.

'I've got... I've got the...' Jozek could hardly speak for sheer joy.

'What have you got?' asked Jozef.

Little Jozek took the manuscript from under his shirt.

And Jozef cried out: 'I must be dreaming, pinch me someone.'

But Jozek did not have to pinch him because Maryla jumped out of bed and did it for him. Jozek was embarrassed and turned away.

Convinced that he was no longer dreaming, Jozef began asking him: 'Where did you get it? How did it happen? Are all the pages here? Did Heniek read it, and did he by any chance show it to the teacher or to someone else?' and so on.

Jozek answered, and became so sure of himself that he said, 'If Heniek hadn't given it back to me, I'd have taken it away from him. Obviously Heniek didn't read it, and even if he did, he wouldn't have understood it because he's so dumb.'

'Dumb he may be,' Maryla put in, 'but he was smart enough to understand that you had stolen his biography.'

Jozef did not answer, for just at that moment
inspiration came to him (page 72)

That Jozek could not explain, but he was sure all the same that Heniek had not shown the manuscript to anyone, not even to the teacher, because Heniek never told on anyone, that's how he was.

'Perhaps,' said the Critic, who had just come in, 'but I believe your joy, my dear colleague, to be unfounded and premature.'

Jozef did not answer, for just at that moment inspiration came to him. So he took Jozek by the hand and they both went to the park. There were plenty of free benches this time, because all the children were at school. They went to write the next episode of their story, that is, the adventure with the manuscript.

Meanwhile, Maryla and the Critic were having tea together, and eating the sandwiches made by Jozef, who, in his joy, had forgotten that he had had no breakfast.

'I have very grave misgivings,' said the Critic. 'All this will finish badly.'

'Big deal,' said Maryla, 'just normal trouble for people with biographies. I'd be in seventh heaven if I had troubles like these.'

'I don't understand what you are talking about,' the Critic was surprised.

'Don't you? I'm saying that I don't have any biography at all, and without a biography you can't be a writer. That's why I have to write an anti-novel.'

'You are still young, you have a long life ahead of you,' said the Critic, trying to reassure her. 'You'll have time to acquire a biography.'

'Perhaps,' said Maryla, 'but if not, then I'll steal one from someone else.'

'Stop talking rubbish,' the Critic said indignantly. 'For pranks like that you could be expelled from the Young Writers' Circle and even end up in prison.'

'I was just wondering what I could do to get there.'

'You have gone mad!' said the Critic. 'What's got into you?'

'I'm not mad at all. A prisoner's biography is highly prized these days, especially in the West. They give you asylum and newspaper publicity right away.'

The Critic said nothing because he did not want Maryla to carry on a conversation which he would have to mention in a report to Party House.

There was a thud from behind the wall and the Critic was startled.

'Oh, that's nothing,' said Maryla. 'One of the Professor's books probably dropped from its shelf. He's always examining history.'

The Critic calmed down and Maryla continued, 'It's Satan's old Professor. He was put in prison because he was reactionary. Things have changed, so he's been released, and he's examining history's maladies again. When they freed him, the Professor went to his villa — the one where the local courtroom is now — but Satan didn't let him in, because he couldn't remember the Professor, and didn't have a little Satan to remind him of the old days. You see, like me, he doesn't have a biography, but it's different with him. Actually, he doesn't really need one since he doesn't have to write novels. When I say I have no biography, that doesn't mean I don't remember what I was like before I grew up, that doesn't mean I don't have a little Marylka. But little Marylka was not Jewish, could not take part in peeing contests, and did not even run away from home. Nor did anything much happen around Marylka. There were no partisans, People's or National. True, Marylka did write compositions on "What I would like to be when I grow up", but there could only be one answer, "super-quota workwoman for the good of our Party";

our teacher would not allow any other answer. That's why I can't write a novel with little Marylka, unless it is about the radiant future, and for that I don't need little Marylka, and anyway I don't want to write about what's going to happen and how good it'll be then.'

Not so Satan. He does not have to write about the past, or foresee what is to come, and that is why he was bound not to remember the Professor and did not remember him.

The Professor felt sad that Satan did not recognize him, and went to look for another place to live. He wandered and searched about for a long time until, at last, the person who snored at night and pottered about during the day in the flat next door to Jozef's, stopped snoring and pottering and died. The Professor moved in there and got rid of the grandfather clock, whose ticking disturbed his examination of history. Jozef was very happy about this because now he could turn off his alarm clock (the one that stood on his bedside table), invite Jozek to his flat, and wait for inspiration. He did not do this for the time being because Maryla distracted him a bit. Only a bit, because Maryla liked to sleep a lot, and she did not snore. She did talk very loudly, but this could be remedied. One day the Professor met Jozef on the stairs, greeted him courteously, and said: 'My dear neighbour, may I take the liberty of asking you kindly to tell your housemaid that she should keep her voice down, as it distracts me from my examination of history.'

Jozef promised, but he was very angry at the Professor for that 'housemaid'. Maryla, however, was not at all offended. On the contrary, she laughed out loud and said, but quietly this time, 'the dear Professor. Only he appreciates me and sees the human being in me. I must make friends with him. Maybe he'll advise me how to get a decent biography.'

And that night Jozef dreamed that Maryla and the Reactionary Professor placed a bomb under the desk of the Comrade Secretary at Party House, but the bomb did not go off because Major Mazurkiewicz found it.

Chapter 9
THE AVIARY

'It must be a miracle! Jozef!' Major Mazurkiewicz exclaimed and embraced Jozef warmly. 'Shoot me, if it is not you, you old horse!'

It happened in a restaurant where Jozef was about to order braised beef because it was time for a meal. At any other time, Jozef would have been very frightened at such an encounter. He had always been afraid of meeting the Major and had done everything to avoid him. He had comforted himself that, even if the Major did see him, then Jozef with his bald head and his moustache in no way resembled his old self from the yard. But now, after the manuscript had been in the Major's hands, Jozef felt only a little uneasy, and even pleased when Major Mazurkiewicz, the first-ranking person in the state after the Comrade Secretary, was so moved by this meeting with an old school friend.

The Major took Jozef's arm and said, 'Let's move, we won't find it very comfortable here,' and led him to a small, separate room set aside for special guests. 'A thousand summers, a thousand winters! Where on earth have you been? Why didn't you get in touch with me?' the Major went on without interruption.

And Jozef was a little surprised that the Major did not know anything about him and was talking as if he really had not heard anything of him since the time they played together in the same yard.

'There's a lot I could tell you,' he wanted to say 'Major' and he just said, 'but you must have heard something about me.'

'Not a thing,' said the Major. 'I figured you were either dead or roaming around in the West somewhere. I heard of one Hirszfeld living in Paris and wrote to him immediately, hoping it was you, but it turned out to be somebody else, don't even think he was a relative of yours.'

'I've changed my name,' said Jozef. 'My name is now Potoczek.'

'Potoczek?! Potoczek?! So it's your literary pseudonym? So you are Jozef Potoczek, the famous writer Jozef Potoczek?! What an idiot I am! Not recognize Jozef Potoczek immediately! Even kids in school know him! No, I can't forgive myself that.'

'You're exaggerating, you can't exactly say I'm famous. I'm just like any other writer in the service of the Party, that's all,' said Jozef modestly. 'And you, with so many state matters on your mind, why should you worry about not recognizing one of the Party rank and file.'

Apparently it dawned on the Major himself that a person of his pre-eminence would not be underlining the eminence of the writer Potoczek, because he said 'so many responsibilities on my mind, so much to do, that I have become completely out of touch with literature.' And wagging his finger playfully at Jozef, he added, 'It's not very nice, not very nice of you, not to have dropped in to see me, that you forgot...'

'How could I have bothered you,' Jozef interrupted, 'I know full well what responsibilities you carry on your shoulders'.

'All the same,' said the Major, 'one should not forget one's old friend. As for my work, you know as well as I, that today I am standing guard, tomorrow it will be someone else. The command post remains, but it is not always the same person in command. Me at present, but later, who knows? With you it's a different matter. You're in command in literature and even when you don't want to or can't, you will always be a part of literature.'

'And you a part of history,' reciprocated Jozef.

And he was very astonished that the Major had called himself a commander so openly when everyone knows – the Major best of all – who commands the Party and the State. Who else but the Secretary at Party House whose right-hand the Major was? Jozef had heard more than once that the Major wanted to become Secretary, but that he should say this so openly?

The waiter served vodka, salmon, caviar and steak tartare, and asked whether His Excellency the Major would desire anything more. The Major waved him aside as if brushing off a fly, and the waiter disappeared behind the door in obeisance.

'... so much to do, that I have become
completely out of touch with literature' (page 78)

'Don't waste your time,' said the Critic, 'because you may never again get another chance like this. Take the bull by the horns and clarify this matter of the manuscript.'

Jozef took the advice, emptied his glass in honour of the reunion, and began. 'Look, Henryk. I'm writing a story about our yard and about ourselves. You know this because you've had the manuscript. Well, I would very much like to ask you if you would tell me frankly what you think of it. You know how it is. A writer often gets carried away by his imagination, even by certain hard to control feelings which he should not permit himself, having always in mind the interest of the Party. That is why your advice will be particularly valuable to me, and will be not only helpful, but even decisive.'

The Major reflected for a moment, drank up his second glass and chased it with a caviar sandwich.

'Wait, wait... yes, I do remember something. Ah, yes, I know,' and he laughed somewhat abashed. 'Forgive me,' he said, 'I hadn't the least idea whose manuscript it was. What an idiot I am. Had I known, I would have dropped everything and read it, but at the time I had merely been irritated that the secrets of a writer's drawer had been tampered with, and I ordered the manuscript to be returned immediately. It was returned, wasn't it?'

'Of course,' confirmed Jozef. 'But what a pity, because I'd like you very much to read it,' he lied.

'Excellent,' whispered the Critic.

'That would be a great honour for me, Jozef. My time is at your disposal. I am at your service. Drop in on me at home one day.'

Then they talked for a while about this and that, the old and the new, finished off their first bottle and began a second, ate roast duck with apple stuffing, then drank coffee and cognac, until at last the Major summoned his car, took Jozef home, and went on to a meeting.

Jozef lay down because his head was hurting a little, and fell asleep.

The Major was sitting next to him in the car and said to the chauffeur, 'stop for a moment in front of my house, I'd like to leave an order.' They drove up to the villa, where a very reactionary minister had once lived. The chauffeur gave a signal and the Major opened the door but did not get out of the car. The duty officer ran up to him and reported, as was required by regulations. The Major ordered him to summon the head-keeper of the aviary. The officer saluted and a moment later the headkeeper was standing before the Major.

'How many magpies do you have ready?' asked the Major.

'One hundred and fifty-four at your command, Comrade Major.'

'Very good. Release forty-three from their cages immediately. They are to carry in their tails the following communiqué:...'

'Yes, Comrade Major,' said the headkeeper, and in a whisper he began repeating after the Major the words of the communiqué so as to forget nothing, since writing down such matters on paper had been strictly forbidden.

'The Comrade Secretary at Party House' the Major dictated, and the headkeeper repeated in a whisper, 'has found that the manuscript of the story by writer Jozef Potoczek contains false information dangerous to our Party, has ordered the manuscript in question to be seized and the writer arrested. Major Mazurkiewicz, however, did not carry out this order. He recognized that this order was contrary to the Constitution because it infringed writers' rights to freedom of expression. The Comrade Secretary acceded to the Major's suggestion and the writer Potoczek remains at liberty.'

'Carry this out immediately — dismissed,' said the Major.

He slammed the car door and hardly had the car started when a swarm of magpies with communiques in their tails rose over the city, scattered in all possible directions, and before Major Mazurkiewicz arrived in his car at the great building where he had his office, and where there was now to be a meeting, the telephone rang in Jozef's room.

'How are you, my friend,' said the Bearded Chairman on the phone. 'How are things?'

'Everything as usual,' replied Jozef.

'I heard that you had some problems.'

'I always have problems.'

'I'm not talking about that. I heard that you got into trouble, but that it turned out to be no more than a scare.'

'Something like that. Nothing worth talking about.' Jozef, having been jolted out of his sleep, was in no mood to confide in the Bearded Poet, and besides that, he disliked talking on the telephone.

'What's bothering you? Surely everything ended up all right. It looks as if we old veterans come out on top again. You can imagine my satisfaction when I heard — and the source was very reliable, one that I've tested more than once — about this scrap over you.'

'What scrap?' said an amazed Jozef.

'Oh, don't you know?'

And the Bearded Poet in a way that only they could understand (or at least the Bearded Poet thought so) told him the latest news that had just reached him. 'He's a great fellow, I've always said so. He won't let anyone get at us.'

Jozef rudely pushed aside the Critic, who was clinging to the receiver to hear what the Bearded Poet was saying, and who was whispering something in Jozef's other ear that he could not make out.

'And another thing,' said the voice in the receiver, 'Maczka will come to you tomorrow. Have a chat with him. He demands that we protest against censorship and against the sentence they piled on him.'

'Is he mad or what?' Jozef exclaimed. 'They kept him less than a week! He's at liberty, not even expelled from the Union, and as for the three years they gave him, so what? Nobody's made him actually serve them. And what has censorship got to do with it?'

'Plenty, he says. If he had been published here, he would never have published anything abroad and all this wouldn't have happened.'

'I won't talk to him,' Jozef tried to interrupt.

'As you wish. You know best, but I have reasons to believe that this thing about censorship was suggested by... you understand?'

'No, I don't.'

'Oh, what a fool. Him, you know who, don't you? Your liberator. Surely you've heard that he wasn't too keen to bury Maczka. Now you understand? Both you and Maczka owe everything to him. So you'd better have a chat with Maczka and think things over. Well, I have to hang up or I'll be late for the meeting with the Major... Bye for now, old friend. Take care.'

'That Maczka's fantastic,' said Maryla, who was just wondering whether to go to the café in her tight skirt, or her jeans, which were tighter still, because she had no other choice.

'You talked to him?' asked Jozef.

'He bought me a coffee yesterday and told me what he said to the Secretary from Party House who was trying to make him ask for a pardon. He said, "I'm not going to allow them to pardon me".'

'What idiotic big-talk. He's trying to turn himself into a hero,' replied Jozef.

'I don't think so,' Maryla decided on the jeans. 'With this arrest and this sentence, which they won't carry out, they've only made fools of themselves. You must have heard what happened in the cell.'

'Yes, I have, but that's just another of Maczka's inventions.'

'No, it isn't. I know for a fact that Maczka did not want to leave his cell. He tore up the plea for a pardon they were trying to trick him into signing and made such a big scene that, if it weren't for the Major, who knows how it would've ended. He talked to Maczka for hours, explained how things were, and drove him home in his own car, in great state. I'm ready. Let's go.'

'I don't feel like it, Maryla. I'll stay home. I've got a headache,' said Jozef, and he stretched himself out on his bed.

'As you like. In that case, I'll take the keys,' and Maryla left.

And Jozef thought a little, dozed a little, until at last he went to sleep, but there wasn't enough time for him to dream because Maryla came back.

Chapter 10
GOLDBERG

A man derives his knowledge from various sources, for
instance from books, newspapers, personal observations,
confidences, gossip, reports, and so on. But how did
Michal Goldberg know that Jozef Potoczek used to be
Jozef Hirszfeld? Perhaps he recognized him by his voice
or perhaps by his face when, after more than twenty
years, he saw the famous writer.

With Jozef Potoczek it was another matter. His tooth
ached badly. He sat in the dentist's chair which the
young assistant pointed him to, closed his eyes, and

opened them only when he heard, 'Dr. Goldberg is wanted on the telephone.' He recognized Goldberg at once, but as he didn't want to be recognized himself, he pretended not to.

Michal Goldberg responded in kind. He pulled out Jozef's tooth, wrote the name Jozef Potoczek into the register, and did not so much as bat an eyelid to suggest that he knew who it really was. It was none of his business that a person preferred to be Potoczek rather than Hirszfeld, and if that were the case then probably he would not want to be recognized at all, or to be reminded of the old days. Goldberg did not remind him, and Jozef, just in case, went to another dentist when he had to have a tooth capped. And they saw each other no more.

Then suddenly — it was in a café — Goldberg approached Jozef, greeted him politely but in a slightly familiar way, led him over to his table, and said, 'Now that everything has finally been clarified and you are Hirszfeld again,' he said this rather loudly and the people around could hear, 'I can't deny myself the pleasure of jogging the memory of an old friend.'

Jozef wanted to say, 'I'm sorry, sir, but there must be some mistake, you must be confusing me with someone else,' but he held himself in check. This impudent Goldberg could become even louder, so Jozef proposed that they sit at a table in a bay window, where no one could sit next to them. It was with difficulty that he controlled his anger, for he would have gladly punched this intruder, but that would have been unbecoming, so instead he smiled a little crookedly and said, 'What a surprise! I wouldn't have dreamed I'd ever see you again in my life.'

'And I could never have guessed it was you,' lied Goldberg. 'You've changed so much, unrecognizable,

'And I could never have guessed it was you,' lied Goldberg
(page 86)

if it weren't that I heard with my own ears that Hirszfeld is Potoczek.'

'I'm not quite sure what you're talking about,' said Jozef, surprised.

Goldberg did not believe that Jozef was surprised, but just in case, he pretended that he was surprised as well.

'What?!' he exclaimed. 'They're all writing about it. I was listening to Western Radio last night. They quoted some London newspaper, I don't remember which one exactly, and said that the famous writer Jozef Hirszfeld, writing under the pseudonym Jozef Potoczek — those were their very words, the ones which caught my ear — Jozef Hirszfeld had spoken out in defence of Greek democrats and sent a telegram to...'

Jozef did not listen to the rest of Goldberg's news, as he was feeling alternately hot and cold as if he were gripped by the flu, and he had to control himself, so as not to let Goldberg notice that he almost spilled his coffee, which he no longer felt like drinking. He looked at his watch and said, 'I'm very sorry, but I'm already late. Please phone me — the best time is in the evening when I am at home. Then we can arrange to get together.'

He shook hands with Goldberg and left quickly.

'Listen,' said Jozek, who had just started his first year in Stefan Batory Secondary School, 'I'd like to write about how we elected our Class Council. It's very interesting and I'm sure you'll like it.'

'I'd rather write first,' said Jozef, 'about the way you passed the school entrance examination.'

'Why? Do you want everyone to know that I copied all my sums off of Goldberg, that I couldn't solve any of the word puzzles, and that, if I had not been saved by my imagination, as the teacher later explained to my mother, I would have failed. No, I don't want to write about that. Or perhaps you want to persuade me to write something that isn't true again, like before about Heniek.'

'You keep bringing that up,' Jozef pretended to be angry, 'but surely I've explained to you that a writer has a right to use fiction.'

'He has a right, I know that,' said Jozek, still unconvinced, 'but I don't want a repeat with someone else's biography, like Goldberg's for instance.'

'I'm sure it won't happen again,' promised Jozef. 'Goldberg's biography is of no interest to a writer.'

'Why is that?' asked Jozek, 'Is it because Goldberg is also a Jew?'

Jozef did not reply. But he frowned a little because the tooth that Goldberg had pulled out was aching.

'Well, what now then? Shall we write about our Council?' Jozek insisted.

'All right,' sighed Jozef.

In our class, a little less than half are Jews. I don't know everyone yet, only Artek, Wilek, Goldberg, a friend from junior school, and Antek from our yard, who is not a Jew.

Our homeroom teacher, the physics master, said that it would be best if the Council Chairman were either myself, because I don't monkey around, or Goldberg, because he did best on the exams. I didn't know how I should respond. I wanted to be Chairman very much, but I was ashamed to admit it. Probably Goldberg was ashamed too, because he kept quiet as well. The teacher became impatient and said, 'When you agree between yourselves, then tell me.'

'Well, maybe you'll be the one,' said Goldberg to me.

'If you like, but maybe it had better be you,' I replied.

And just then Antek walked up to us.

'The best thing would be to make Antek our Chairman,' I then said.

'What Chairman?' he asked.

'The Chairman of our Class Council,' I said.

'Great. If you want me, then I'll be your Chairman.' Antek agreed straight away, kicked his ball, and ran off.

'What's the matter, are you crazy? What sort of Chairman is that? He's too stupid!' Goldberg shouted at me.

'That's just it. He's stupid so he'll make a good Chairman. He lives in my tenement and will listen to us,' I explained to Goldberg.

And he replied, 'Not us, but you. You're slippery as a snake. I won't let you copy from me any more.'

And he was so mad at me that he stopped speaking to me. Artek, Wilek, and the other boys were all talked into it however, and Antek became Chairman. He was certainly stupid, that Antek, but he never hit me, and he never called me a Jew, like Heniek did. And I preferred him as Chairman to that old brain-box Goldberg.

'You've written a little too much about that,' Jozef interrupted, 'let me.'

And Jozef began to write. But not for long. He heard someone approach him laughing loudly.

'Ah, it's you, my dear colleague. Something seems to have amused you.'

'Very much indeed,' answered the Critic, for it was his loud laughter that had disturbed Jozef's writing.

'And what is it, may I ask?'

'I've just come from Party House,' said the Critic, explaining his cheerfulness, 'where I read in a Western Press bulletin that the famous writer Jozef Hirszfeld, writing under the pseudonym of Jozef Potoczek, the same person who came to the defence of the Greek democrats, has been dismissed from the Writers' Union because, during a search of his home, there was found the manuscript of a new novel in which he attacks state anti-Semitism...'

'Well, what's so funny about that? That's slander! Outright provocation!' Jozef said angrily.

'I am laughing,' said the Critic, who was serious now, 'because you, my dear colleague, have more luck than sense. In this brazen accusation of anti-Semitism against our government, which you rightly describe as provocation, a priceless service has been rendered you. I have found out from a friendly comrade at Party House that the Comrade Secretary really did want to have you expelled from the Union for those machinations with the questionnaire, but when he read what they were writing about you in the West, he changed his mind. And in my opinion, you should as proof of your gratitude immediately and in public condemn these, as you rightly called them, slanders.'

'And if I were in your place,' said Maryla, 'I wouldn't let such a splendid opportunity go by and would send your manuscript to the West right now. Just imagine the publicity they'll give you! They'll translate you into every language and give you a prize.'

'You've gone completely mad,' said Jozef in anger.

'Maryla, you don't realize what you're saying,' echoed the Critic.

'You two go together like an old pair of shoes,' said Maryla and she began painting her fingernails brown, as violet was now out of fashion. 'You're incapable of learning anything, even with Maczka as an example.'

'What about Maczka! He's just a clown,' Jozef cut back.

'Clown!' Maryla was rather angry now. 'Then listen to what I found out. Some foreign correspondents approached Maczka and asked him for an interview. Maczka pretended he was ill, apologized to them, and asked them to come back in a few days. And do you know why he did that? He did it to gain time and to get the advice of those who matter. And I can only guess who. When he'd been advised, he finally refused to give an interview, and for that he's been promised a yearly trip to Italy, where he will write some trashy book about heroism and martyrdom, for which, you can be sure, he will receive a national award.'

'Rubbish! I don't know anything about this,' Jozef made a wry face to show his contempt.

'Phone the Bearded Poet. Then you'll know.'

And Jozef phoned. But the Bearded Poet only said, 'Not now. But drop in to see me some time and I'll explain everything to you,' and hung up.

Jozef was very puzzled. The Bearded Poet was Chairman, that's true, but he, Jozef, was the Secretary, and everybody knew what that meant. So why did the Bearded Poet make a decision without him, and why did he, the Secretary of the Party Branch, know nothing of what was happening to Maczka, and have to be told about it by Maryla?

And while he was puzzling it over Jozek continued to write about how Antek, who had become Chairman through him, now began plotting against him and even called him a 'chicken Jew' during recess.

The Critic, having sneaked a look at what little Jozek had written, said to Jozef, 'Twice now you have got away with it. The first time with that damned questionnaire, the second with that manuscript that was returned to you and for which you weren't called to account. But don't push your luck. I advise you to be very careful.'

'Why does he always interrupt me?' Jozek complained.

But big Jozef, instead of taking the little one's side, only said, 'You should go home now, Jozek, your mother will be getting worried. It's late.'

And he himself went to a café for a drink. On the way, he looked up at the sky because he imagined that the flock of magpies was circling over the city again, and that the sparrows on the rooftops were twittering rather loudly. He went into the café and ordered a single vodka. He drank it, ordered a second, paid, and returned home to make some coffee, as the coffee in the café was vile.

'Congratulations,' Maryla greeted him. 'The Bearded Poet phoned and told me to tell you that you should submit an application for sick leave, because you are exhausted and are suffering from insomnia and neurosis. You are to go to a sanatorium. Everything has been arranged with Party House. Oh yes, and he said your place will be taken by an editor, the one from the "Literary Gazette".'

Jozef did not reply. He only lay down, and for a long, long time he could not go to sleep. And when he did fall asleep at last, he was not haunted by any dream.

The next morning, Maryla asked him, 'What did you dream last night?'

'Nothing,' replied Jozef.

'That's impossible,' said Maryla. 'That I never get any dreams, that is understandable, but you, with such a biography!'

Chapter 11
WHERE DO ALL THESE JEWS COME FROM?

Jozef hardly stirred out of his flat. He went out only
once to arrange his train ticket and his admission to
the sanatorium, and on his way he dropped into the
patisserie, as he had promised Maryla some cakes.

'The moth heads for the flame', it is said, but no one
knows what the moth does when there is no flame.
When Jozef Potoczek was merely Jozef Potoczek and no
one else, and that was for many years, he was sometimes
puzzled that he never came across any of his old friends
who might have recognized someone else in him. True,

The Critic, having sneaked a look at what little Jozek
had written, said to Jozef... (page 92)

it did happen with Goldberg, but that was only once and does not count. But no sooner had Jozef Potoczek begun recognizing Jozef Hirszfeld in himself when various people suddenly came at him out of nowhere, like those moths at the flame, to greet the Hirszfeld in Potoczek. First that Mazurkiewicz, then Goldberg again, and now the two at once, Meller and Rosenovna, today probably Mellerova, from the way they were sitting together in the café where Jozef had come for the cakes it was immediately obvious that they were a married couple. Jozef knew of their existence, and they of his, but somehow they kept missing each other. And now it was the same story as with Goldberg. Jozef was not a redhead, balding rather. He did not wear a red tie or even a fiery glance, so why then did all these moths start flying at him?

Jozef had barely managed to get away from the Mellers, and had not yet even had time to hail a taxi, when he ran into Levin. He knew that Levin was now Lewikowski, that he had served in the army, had even been a Colonel, and had pretended that he did not recognize Jozef. Or maybe he really had not reconized him and recognized him only now? Anyway, he greated Jozef heartily, and took off his hat, as he was in civilian clothes and was again called Levin. He took Jozef by the arm and said, 'Come on, I want to talk to you.'

Jozef wanted to apologize that he had no time, he was busy, maybe another time, but Levin would not listen.

'I know, I know it all, ' he said, 'it's no use pretending any more. We're hanging together on the same branch, you and I. We have done the dirty work and now we can go. Don't think that I am surprised by this, or that I feel any regret. Not at all. New cadres have grown — national cadres. I understand this, for I was and am a Communist. But what I don't understand is why, instead of letting us depart in honour, they are trying to pull us to pieces.'

And Levin started to tell his story, how he hadn't been retired with the rank of general, as he deserved, hadn't been given a full pension, had been refused a permit to go abroad for medical care, and, on the whole, had been treated in a churlish way by the Party as well.

Jozef listened, or rather he pretended to listen, and was just about to bid Levin good-bye, when they ran across Rowinski, now Rosenthal again. He had worked for some time in the judiciary and, it was said, had rendered the 'appropriate' services. Later he spent some time working at Party House, but now, because he had no degree, he had been relegated to housing administration. And when was he supposed to have studied? While eliminating the enemies of the Party perhaps? Then no one asked for a degree, and now...

'Anyway, what more can I say? After all, Jozef, you yourself have been kicked out of the censorship office, so you know well enough what they have done to us.'

Jozef snorted angrily. He did not like to be reminded of his work in the censorship office, and said, 'Nobody kicked me out. I left of my own free will.'

Rosenthal laughed. 'You always were naive,' he said, 'and naive you always will be. You think that because you're a writer nobody can touch you. Stop kidding yourself. They have enough writers of their own, and when they no longer need you, they'll get rid of you too. You know very well how it's done. Just one telephone call and Hirszfeld, sorry, Potoczek, the writer, does not exist and never did exist. And what will you do then? Breed minks, like me, perhaps? After all, you've got to make a living somehow.'

Rosenthal wanted to say something more, but just then Lieutenant-Colonel Cukrowski passed by, now probably Cukerman again, as before, because he greeted them with a loud 'Hello, Hevra!' and smiled mysteriously but fortunately did not come up to them.

'He shouldn't be so cheerful,' Levin observed. 'There's little to stop him from being put on trial. And what for? For loyal service, such are the times. Supposedly righting the wrongs of the past.'

Jozef had had enough of this talk, so he pretended to be in a great hurry and took his leave. He got in a taxi, where the Critic was already seated, and gave directions to be taken home.

'What are you doing, my dear colleague?' said the Critic reproachfully. 'That Levin, and Rosenthal, and that whole motley crew, they're dangerous people, all closely watched by the Major. And who knows if they're not secretly working for him. Their every word is heard clearly. Arrange that vacation as soon as possible, otherwise you can only bring more trouble down on your head.'

Jozef said nothing, but he directed the cab driver to take him not to his flat but to the Ministry of Health, where he had been promised admission to the sanatorium.

Maryla, who had waited in vain for her cream cakes and was therefore angry with Jozef, went to see the Professor.

He greeted her politely, offered her some coffee, and even wanted to show her the third volume of The History of Jewish Martyrology, but they were interrupted by the Critic. He picked up the volume which the Professor had only just taken down from the shelf, looked at the introduction written by the Professor, and said, 'You have performed a great task here, Professor. Those unfortunates who remained alive should be grateful to you for this historical truth.'

'Unfortunately,' replied the Professor, 'it is that very gratitude which they have forgotten. What is more, and it is a sad thing to say, they repay those who once rescued them with black ingratitude and slander the good name of our nation.'

'I don't understand,' said Maryla. 'Why is that?'

The Professor smiled mysteriously and said, 'My dear young lady, I envy you that ignorance.'

'But Professor,' said Maryla with pretended anger, 'everyone tells me that I am ignorant, everyone even envies me that, and they all invoke the fact that I am young. So what am I to do? I'm not bright, I have no biography, so what sort of writer can I be? Maybe I should go to a department store and sell? I even tried that once, but they closed for stock taking.'

'The Professor had no intention,' interrupted the Critic, 'of undermining your faith in your own powers, Maryla, and...'

'Of course not, nothing could be further from my mind,' confirmed the Professor, 'and I am always ready to give you the benefit of my advice and experience, whenever you should desire it of me.'

And while he was saying this, someone knocked at the door. It was Jozek. He was looking for big Jozef because he had something very important to tell him. The Critic immediately started to ask what Jozek wanted to tell big Jozef, but Jozek only called 'Bye-bye' and ran off again. He met Jozef climbing the stairs and together they went into Jozef's flat, where there was no longer an alarm clock, as Maryla had decided a long time ago that it would be better that way. At least it would not jangle her nerves, always ringing at the wrong time.

'Guess what I'm going to tell you,' said Jozek.

'Don't know.'

'Well, try.'

'I can't.'

'Gosh, you're thick. Listen, my mother told me in

secret that my father has agreed to move. We're going to live in another tenement now. My mother told me the new address in secret as well. I went to have a look. It's great. And the main thing is I'll be rid of Heniek at last. I also found out that it's nearly all Jews living there.'

'Who told you that?'

'What do you mean, who? I read all the name-plates on the doors.'

Jozef smiled sadly, gave Jozek all the cream and cheese cakes that he had bought for Maryla and began to brew some tea so that Jozek would have something to drink with them.

Meanwhile the Critic, who had brazenly stretched out on Jozef's bed, began to snore and mumble something in his sleep, for he had found a cache of documents from which he compiled the fourth volume of The History of The Black Ingratitude of Those Saved from Extermination, and the Comrade Secretary rewarded him with the Chairmanship of the Writers' Union, in place of the Bearded Poet.

Chapter 12
ZIONIST

'I suppose you think I'm happy about your going,' said Maryla.

'You told me so yourself,' said Jozef and he added a few books to his already well-filled suitcase.

'Yes, that's true. I was happy that I would finally be able to sleep to my heart's content, but now I'm not so happy.'

'But why?' asked Jozef.

'Because I've grown quite used to you.'

'Well, you'll now have a chance to grow less used.'

Jozef pressed the suitcase lid down with his knee, but could not make it shut.

'Thank you, but I won't take advantage of it. You'd better give these books to me, I'll put them in my bag.'

'I have no intention of taking that bag with me,' Jozef went on struggling with his own suitcase.

'But I have.'

Jozef looked at Maryla in amazement.

'Why do you stare at me as though you'd never seen me before? I'm going with you,' and Maryla began to toss various odds and ends from her bedside table into her travel bag.

'That's impossible,' Jozef protested. 'I have an admittance for only one.'

'I'll admit myself. I'll find myself a small room, and milk bars are everywhere. All we have to do is buy some smoked sausage on the way to the station.'

'I don't even have a ticket for you,' Jozef said defensively.

'That doesn't matter. If we can't get one in the ticket office, I'll go without it. Just have some money ready to pay the fine.'

Jozef said nothing. He merely took the books out of his suitcase and put them into Maryla's bag. And he was so taken up with his packing that he failed to notice Rabinowicz, who was standing in the doorway loaded down with parcels.

'That's exactly how I imagined Jozef Hirszfeld,' he said. 'You haven't changed a bit.'

He threw the parcels down on the bed and heartily embraced Jozef who stood there nonplussed. He had been certain that Artur Rabinowicz was dead. He had lost sight of him at the beginning of the war, and here... what a shock!

'Formerly Rabinowicz, now Rabinowicz, in a word,

always and incorrigibly Rabinowicz,' Artur introduced himself and kissed Maryla's hand, winking at Jozef, which was supposed to mean, or so at least Jozef understood, that nothing had happened to make him change his name.

The room was in such a mess that Maryla did not know where to seat her guest. But he was not concerned with that, he only said, 'Take no notice of me, just carry on packing. No need to hurry.'

'Do forgive me, Artur, but I didn't know... the train leaves in three hours' time.'

'Forget the train,' interrupted Rabinowicz. 'We can do without it. I'll drive you there in my car. I'm at your service,' and he asked Maryla to see to the cognac which was also at the service of long lost friends.

While they were talking little Jozek slipped into the room, and the inseparable Critic behind him. And it became as crowded as a tram in rush hour.

Little Jozek was about to run off because he didn't like crowds but big Jozef said, 'You know what, Jozek, we'll take you with us as well. You are likely to be in the way when your parents move into the new tenement, and you have a few days left till the end of the school year. As it is, you were intending to play truant with Artek until then anyway.'

'You've guessed right,' said Jozek. 'All right, I'll go with you but I have to tell Artek first.'

Jozek said this because he probably had not recognized Rabinowicz. How could he when the other had grown up and was standing with his back towards him whispering something in Maryla's ear.

'Do you know what I just found out?' Jozek asked suddenly.

'No.' Jozef was helping Maryla pour the cognac into glasses.

'I've just found out, but it's a secret remember, that Artek is a Zionist.'

'Who told you that?'

'He told me so himself,' Jozek replied.

'At last,' said Maryla, 'at last I'm going to find out what a Zionist is, and from the most dependable source, from you,' and she turned to Rabinowicz.

'It isn't possible to explain it all in one go. But I'll try. First,' began Rabinowicz, 'every Zionist must be a Jew, but that certainly doesn't mean that every Jew, like me for instance, must be a Zionist.'

'How's that?' Maryla was surprised and a little disillusioned, 'I was sure you were a Zionist, and a real one at that.'

'I was, I was, my dear lady,' Rabinowicz winked at the Critic this time, 'I was until I found out what it meant to be a Zionist, but when I did find out I stopped being one and am not one now. Secondly,' Rabinowicz went on, 'a Zionist is one who belongs to the Masonic Lodge of International Jewish Capital. You know, that's the same lodge thanks to which Hitler seized power, unleashed war and organized the purge of Jews...'

'You're pulling my leg,' Maryla pretended to be angry.

'Not at all, dear lady. The Jews thought we needed a purge in order to get rid of those amongst us who were, as they put it today, weak and infirm elements. And those who emerged revived and stronger after that bloodbath are now, and only now, capable of ruling the world. Thirdly, Zionist is the Jewish synonym for the word "patriot". Obviously it is possible to be a patriot and not a Zionist but let's say a Communist, like you, sir, to take an example,' here Rabinowicz turned to the Critic. 'However, it is even possible, if one wishes it, to be a Zionist-Communist...'

'This is too much,' the Critic said nervously, 'those

are two completely irreconcilable concepts.'

'No matter,' said Rabinowicz, 'because with good will — on both sides, of course — it is easy to link them through patriotism. It's so simple that even Miss Maryla will recognize...'

'Why "even"?' Maryla flashed.

'Sorry,' Rabinowicz corrected himself, 'not "even" but "only".'

'And why "only"?' Jozef asked.

'I'll tell you that in the car,' Rabinowicz interrupted. 'It's time to go, my friends.'

Maryla sat next to Rabinowicz with a box of chocolates on her lap. In the back seat of the comfortable Fiat Jozef sat on one side, the Critic on the other, and little Jozek in between, also with a box of chocolates on his lap. He put a couple of sheets of exercise paper on the box, leaned forward so the Critic could not peek at what he was doing, and began to write about how Artek who was called Boxer because he was the strongest in the class took on and dealt with the whole Tolek Kapuscinski gang.

Tolek, wrote little Jozek, was not at all strong, but he had a gang and the boys in the gang wore Fascist sword badges on their lapels.

One day Artek went up to Tolek and said, 'I have a great favour to ask you.'

'What favour?' asked Tolek.

'If you don't mind, I'd like you to keep your badge at home.'

Tolek made a wolf-whistle with two fingers, he always managed to get it right, and his gang came running up straight away. This happened in the street, not far from our school. Nearly the whole class, nearly all the Jews as well, crowded round, except that nobody was in a hurry to help Artek.

I thought Artek would make off, for what else could he do? There were twice as many of us Jews, but I knew that none of them were too eager for a battle. I was angry at my Jewish friends, they were always like that. First in sucking up to the teacher, first to the blackboard, but last when it came to standing up for a friend. Not like Tolek's gang. Always in unison, always together, especially against Jews. So I was scared for Artek. But he didn't seem to care. He seized Tolek by the lapel, and started removing the sword badge. Then one member of the gang kicked him, and another raised his satchel to hit Artek in the head. Then Artek seized Tolek's arms and swung him around, first one way, then another, with a swish. Tolek's gang jumped back, and then ran off. Then Artek steadied him, and without the least trace of hurry took off his sword badge, gave it to him and said, 'You won't forget to wear it at home, will you?' Then Artek walked off and I followed him. I saw him step into a gateway and wipe his nose which was bleeding.

Rabinowicz's car was now a long way out of town and Maryla had had time to eat half of her box of chocolates, the Critic was snoring as usual, Jozef was dozing as well, and little Jozek had grown tired of writing and turned to his chocolates when suddenly the hitherto silent Rabinowicz spoke up. 'I said "only", Miss Maryla, because only you are a little different from them' — here he indicated with his head Jozef and the Critic, who was listening in furious that they were not letting him sleep — 'and also different from me.'

'Everyone tells me that — that I'm still young and therefore stupid,' said Maryla.

'That you are young is not a sin, and that you are stupid is not true,' continued Rabinowicz. 'And they aren't stupid either, as some might think. It's simply that they have been drawn into a mincer without wishing it, and they have been ground up so effectively that all their bones have been crushed into tiny bits, and they have been let out of that mincer unable to stand on their own feet without a prop. So they prop themselves up with whatever comes their way, a bit of Communism, a bit of patriotism, a bit of cunning, but they feel most comfortable when they are suspended, for then they can even dance when somebody pulls the string.'

'And what about yourself?' asked Maryla.

'Well, I'm just a lucky fellow. Had I gone to the ghetto, then I would certainly have become a Jewish policeman, as there was a great demand for boxers. But I was lucky enough to escape to the East.'

'And so you were saved by the East?' said Maryla, bewildered.

'Not at all,' Rabinowicz protested, 'Not by the East but by a labour camp.'

'So you were in a labour camp? For how long?'

'Not too long, I got fifteen years but I only served eight. Yes, Miss Maryla, I was saved by a labour camp.'

'Why were you locked up?' Maryla's interest was heightened.

'For Ukrainian nationalism and storing arms,' answered Rabinowicz.

'But you're a Jew?' Maryla was perplexed.

'You ask as if it were my fault that I was locked up for Ukrainian nationalism and not for Zionism. I swear to you, it was through no fault of mine. I escaped to the East and I wanted to join the army. I was a sucker, and when a Jew is a sucker he's the limit. They didn't take me in the army, they had enough of their own. So I thought to myself, I'll get closer to the front, surely there'll be some use for me there. And so there was. I wandered from one commander to another, on the

107

way I lost all my papers, everyone turned me away, until at last one commander took pity on me and locked me up. I was wearing an embroidered Ukrainian shirt but it was embroidered somewhat differently from theirs. I told them I was from the country because I thought a peasant origin would save me. Then they found a scout knife and a few cartridges in my pocket. That did it. I tried to save myself and said that it wasn't true, that I had lied, that I wasn't a Ukrainian but a Jew. Unfortunately, they had no need at that time for Zionists but there has always been a demand for Ukrainian nationalists. And that was that.'

'But you haven't explained to me yet why I'm different.'

'Patience, patience, your turn will come. You are different but only for the time being. You are in the queue for the mincer. They have not yet had time to put you in but don't worry, they will.'

'So what am I to do?'

'What are you to do? You're asking me? If you were mine and not Jozef's I would tell you but like this...'

'Stop confusing her,' said Jozef, 'why don't you tell us what you're doing nowadays.'

'Nothing interesting,' answered Rabinowicz. 'I'm an engineer, I worked in a factory, made a bit on the side, and now I'm sitting quietly and waiting for my exit permit.'

The Critic leaned over to Jozef's ear and whispered, so as not to let Rabinowicz hear, 'A nice state of affairs, isn't it? It seems that lately you have completely lost your bearings. What imprudence! What imprudence!'

'I'm hungry,' said Maryla (the box of chocolates had long been empty), 'and I would like to eat something hot.'

'Right,' said Rabinowicz, and he stopped the car in front of a village tavern they were just passing.

They had some pork loin cutlets but with bread as there was no cabbage left, and they drank lemonade because there was no beer left. Then they drove on and finally reached their destination late in the evening.

Maryla spent the night with little Jozek in a room which she rented from the waitress who served coffee in the sanatorium café. Rabinowicz spent the night in the car because he didn't want to go to the hotel. For Jozef there was a separate room with a balcony and only one bed which, however, was sufficiently large to accomodate both him and the Critic. Everyone was tired and so intoxicated with the fresh air that not one of them dreamed anything that night.

Only it seemed to little Jozek that the man who had brought them here in his Fiat was rather like Artek, the strongest boy in their class. But this man had a false leg as he had lost his real one in the labour camp while felling trees.

Chapter 13
which does not exist because little Jozek is superstitious.

Chapter 14
TWO HOMELANDS

The Jewish War had begun and before Jozef and the others had managed to switch off the radio which was standing on the bedside table the war was over. The Comrade Secretary, not the one at Party House, but the more senior one at the Red House in Moscow, became so concerned about Zionist aggression that he personally phoned the President at the White House in Washington to intervene on behalf of the defeated Arabs.

What it was that they agreed on over the telephone, Jozek did not write down for big Jozef did not tell him, and he had no desire to listen to the Critic's prattle.

The Critic was deeply offended by Jozek. He went for a walk in the forest and — something that had never happened before — he did not invite Maryla to go with him. And while he was walking in the direction of the bridge, and the forest beyond, he saw a postman waving a telegram.

'A telegram from Party House to Citizen Jozef Potoczek,' said the postman because he was very near-sighted and confused the Critic with Jozef.

The Critic took the telegram and opened it because, as we know, he was very inquisitive. He read it through and returned to the sanatorium where Jozef was playing dominoes with Maryla.

'My dear colleague,' the Critic called out, a little short of breath, 'the Comrade Secretary at Party House has summoned you. It is very urgent,' and he gave Jozef the telegram.

'No rush,' said Maryla. 'It's Sunday today, and even Zionists respect the day of rest.'

But Jozef did not listen to Maryla's advice. Instead, he ran up to his room to pack his suitcase. The Critic followed him and Maryla continued with little Jozek the game of dominoes she had started with big Jozef.

'Do you know what we wrote about war in our story?' asked Jozek.

'I knew, but I can't remember,' answered Maryla.

'We wrote that "grown-ups don't like wars...".' Jozek quoted. 'At the time I liked what we wrote very much but I don't like it now and we'll have to change it.'

'Why?' asked Maryla.

'Because sometimes grown-ups do like wars,' Jozek explained, 'especially when you have to defend your homeland.'

'What bull,' interjected Maryla.

And Jozek, very surprised because he did not under-

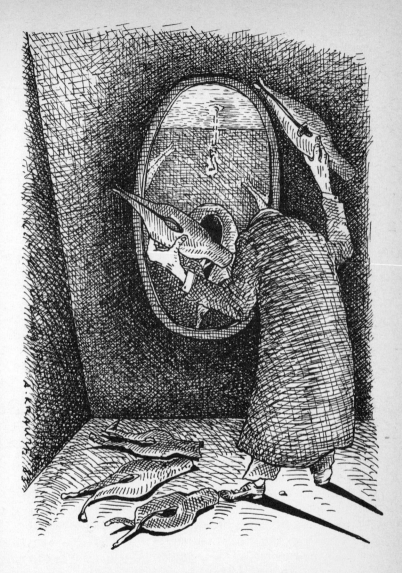

'You're right,' he said. 'We'll have to write that part
a different way' (page 114)

stand what that meant, asked, 'What did you say?'

Maryla laughed and Jozek noticed that she was cheating because she didn't want to lose.

'It's dishonourable to cheat,' he said. 'If you're afraid to lose, then don't play at all, nobody's forcing you.'

'I've learned from the Zionists,' said Maryla. 'They were also afraid to lose, so they attacked the Arabs from behind — that is dishonourable too.'

Jozek was offended with what she said. 'I didn't know that you were anti-Semitic. If they hadn't attacked from behind, the Arabs would have beaten them. It's one thing to cheat in a game of dominoes like you're doing and another to cheat at war when you're defending your homeland,' announced Jozek. 'Anyway, it wasn't cheating, just wartime cunning.'

'If that is the case,' said Maryla, 'then you should cut out of your story what you wrote about David and Goliath.'

Jozek reflected upon this.

'You're right,' he said. 'We'll have to write that part a different way.'

'A pity Rabinowicz isn't here. He would suggest the best way of doing it.'

Maryla wanted to say more but Jozef had come in. He was very angry that they were still playing dominoes instead of getting ready to leave. He swept the dominoes into his pocket and said, 'We are leaving in half an hour's time. The Director has promised us his car so that we can make the train.'

Jozek ran off to pack his fishing rods, while the Critic, who had nothing to pack because he came without a suitcase and wore one of Jozef's shirts when his own got dirty, said to Maryla, 'I'm afraid that this aggression has turned the boy's head. If it goes any further, he'll grow up to be a Jewish chauvinist.'

114

'You're always afraid of something,' Maryla replied. 'You're always nosing after something, and if you weren't constantly writing reports, you'd have a nervous breakdown.'

While she was saying this, Jozef brought in her travel bag, called Jozek, and they all got into the car.

The chauffeur was about to start but a tyre burst and they had to get out.

'A new tube,' said the chauffeur. 'I only put it on yesterday. Not surprising they lost the war, I suppose they were supplied with the same kind of rubbish. With this kind of technology they might as well prepare themselves for the next world, not start up something with Dayan. Give us a hand, son,' he said to Jozek and started pumping up the tyre.

'Why did you say,' Jozek asked, 'that the Arabs got our technology? Is it true?'

'Our technology and our Dayan. The technology and Dayan are both ours, but the technology is post-war People's and Dayan is pre-war — he served here, under our Marshal, you know.' The chauffeur kicked the tyre a few times and said, 'That'll do, we should be able to get to the station now.'

And they drove off.

There were no seats free in the train, except for one whole compartment which was locked. Jozef took the conductor aside because he didn't want the others to see what was changing hands, and the conductor allowed them into the compartment.

Maryla sat by the window, the Critic next to her, and opposite them Jozek sat next to the window with Jozef at his side. They unpacked their provisions, some ham and cheese sandwiches which the sanatorium had given them for lunch, and started eating.

'It's a pity they don't have a restaurant car,' said

Maryla. 'I'd much rather have a bowl of soup and some hot dogs with horseradish.'

'On a hot day like this?' Jozef was surprised.

'Well, so what?' Maryla took the slice of ham out of a sandwich, popped it into her mouth, and threw the bread into the waste paper bin under the window. 'It must be hotter than this in Sinai, but I'm sure nobody there is stuffing himself with dry bread.'

An officer entered the compartment, asked politely if he could take a seat, and before Jozef had time to reply, because Maryla had her mouth full and could not speak, sat down in a corner by the door.

After a moment, someone else came in, asked nothing and sat down opposite the officer immediately covering himself with a newspaper.

Then an elderly lady, who, though she was wearing glasses, did not notice the Critic, turned directly to Maryla and asked her courteously if she would be so kind as to move over a little, after which she placed a basket full of cherries on the seat and sat down next to it.

She was followed in by a spindly young man in jeans and a nylon open-necked shirt, who winked at Maryla and sat down opposite the basket of cherries.

Jozef and the Critic leaned forward to each other and began to talk quietly, so that no one could hear them, about why the Comrade Secretary might be summoning Jozef so urgently.

'Perhaps the editor of the "Literary Gazette" is ill, and there is no one to take his place?' said Jozef.

'I don't think so,' answered the Critic. 'It's more likely that someone has written a report on this Rabinowicz. I warned you...'

'Rubbish!' snorted Jozef. 'Rabinowicz is not a Party member and the Comrade Secretary is not in the least interested in him.'

'They could have arrested him,' insisted the Critic, 'and he could have said something against you.'

'What could they possibly arrest him for?' Jozef still queried.

'For Zionism, profiteering, and dangerous conversations,' answered the Critic.

'Perhaps something happened to the Bearded Poet?' Jozef did not want to hear any more about Rabinowicz.

'Then he would not be summoning you. The Bearded Poet has his own deputy chairman,' said the Critic. 'But, in any case, my dear colleague, if I were you I would study the Comrade Secretary's speech once again, particularly the parts concerning aggression. You should be ready to discuss not only Union problems, but political subjects as well,' and he handed Jozef a newspaper with the latest speech by the Secretary.

Jozef began to study it attentively, and the Critic, as was his habit, dozed off. Not for long, however, because the spindly youngster, who had no idea what to do with his long legs, kicked him in the ankle. The Critic groaned, and the young man said, 'Sorry, I hope I didn't hurt you.' He wore hobnail boots, probably because he liked climbing mountains.

'Excuse me, sir, could I possibly ask you to lend me the Comrade Secretary's speech when you have finished it?' the officer asked Jozef.

Jozef consented with a nod of his head and carried on reading.

'... I only heard it on the radio,' said the officer, 'and I'd like to have it confirmed that the Comrade Secretary has announced the emigration of citizens of Jewish origin.'

'But not until the autumn, surely,' the elderly lady with the glasses spoke up, all the while eating her cherries and spitting the stones into her hand, 'because my partner, and he's a decent man, though a Jew, must have time to settle his accounts with me.'

'You're wrong there, lady,' interrupted the young man, 'if you take my case, I won't even be able to leave by next winter because...'

'You're leaving?' Maryla showed interest.

'I want to,' he answered, 'but I don' t have the right papers and I won't have them for a year, not until my fiancée gets her school certificate.'

'How's that? I don't understand.' Maryla opened a box of sweets and offered them to the young man.

He took a whole handful and said, 'Well, I went to the police station and asked if I could present my emigration papers, so they asked me who was Jewish in my family. I said, I'm sorry but nobody is. Well, then you can't go. So I found myself a fiancée, she's Jewish, but she doesn't want to leave until she's got her certificate, or maybe even a university diploma. I've got no luck.'

'Your fiancée is a practical girl,' observed the officer. 'She knows the value of our degrees in the West. We might be a little behind the United States in the export of manufactured goods, but a number of countries would certainly envy our export in brainpower.'

'That's true,' confirmed the elderly lady, and she threw the stones out of the open window. 'But what I just can't understand is why the authorities allow them to take whatever they want away with them. When I was going on excursion to France, they only let me take a litre of vodka, some smoked sausage, and half a kilo of mushrooms, but these people even take their cars with them. My partner even wants permission to take dollars...'

'Speculation with foreign currency, Madam,' interrupted a newcomer who had been standing inside the compartment door for a few moments, deciding whether to sit next to the basket or the young man in jeans, 'is our economic disease. The only way to cure it is to bring back the death penalty for speculators. I wouldn't use kid gloves with them. Put them behind bars and confiscate all their property. Only then will they understand.'

Jozef could not read and handed the newspaper to the officer, who was in no hurry to read the Comrade Secretary's speech either and put the newspaper on his lap, while the man standing in the doorway came and sat next to him.

'Captain,' he said, 'you are no doubt hurrying to your unit.' And, getting no reply, he continued, 'I don't believe that there is a mobilization, but we must be ready. The Germans succeeded in catching us unawares once, now the Israelis have used German tactics and have got away with it as well, but let them just try to make the third time the charm. We must be on our guard, and above all we must beware of their fifth column. I trust you won't argue with me, sir,' and he tapped the knee of the gentleman sitting in the corner opposite him, who had been covered by a newspaper the whole time, and even now did not stir.

Then he tapped the knee of the young man, who asked, 'Why has it got that number, five?'

'It gets its name from the Fascist Falange of General Franco,' explained the officer.

'Ah, I get it,' said the young man and his hand reached over to Maryla's box for another handful of sweets.

They entered a tunnel, the compartment went black, and they heard Maryla giving the young man a slap, for his hand, having missed the box of sweets, had mistakenly come to rest elsewhere. The tunnel ended, the conductor came in, inspected the tickets, and said to someone standing in the corridor that there was one seat available in the compartment.

A fat gentleman with a long moustache and a sweaty

bald head sat down between Jozef and the young man.

'It's almost beyond belief,' he said, 'how unkind, not to mention ill-bred, our youth is today. I asked you, young man,' and here he turned to the spindly youth beside him, 'if there were not one more seat free in this compartment. And you did not even deign to reply.'

'That's because, according to the by-laws,' answered the young man, 'there is room for three, there were already four of us, and you're the fifth.'

'I am not the fifth,' replied the fat man, 'I'm the fourth.'

(He had probably failed to notice little Jozek who was sleeping curled up by the window.)

'It all comes to the same thing,' the young man disagreed, 'you alone can count as two.'

'What damned impertinence! Unbelievable!' the fat man growled angrily.

'It's the working class at your service,' answered the young man.

'What manners! Not even a bit of respect for grey hair!' The fat man was muttering to himself now, while the sweat poured profusely from his bald head down his forehead.

The officer spread the newspaper out and began to read. He did not read long.

'Excuse me,' he turned to Jozef. 'Could I possibly ask you what is your opinion about the fact that there are still people in our country without a homeland?'

'In this matter,' answered the Critic who did not want Jozef to reply, 'as in all other matters, I completely share the opinion of the Comrade Secretary.'

But Jozef, who was furious with the tall young man who was trying to score with Maryla, with the fat man who was comfortably leaning against him, and with the elderly lady who had covered him with cherry stones

120

when she tried to throw them out of the window, took out his anger on the officer, and said, 'Please read the article more carefully. The Comrade Secretary does not speak of people without a homeland, but of those with two homelands.'

'You know, that's just like my cousin, my uncle's son,' the elderly lady interjected. 'He's got two passports at the same time, ours and a Russian one, and that's why he can go to Sochi every year for a vacation. But he said to me once, "I'd give them both away for an American one!" '

'Before the First World War, the English had no passports at all,' added the fat man. 'A nation with such an advanced culture does not need to be looked after; it has its own internal discipline, which we can only envy.'

'Envy the English?' the man who had formerly stood in the doorway of the compartment and demanded the rope for speculators, expressed his surprise. 'Perhaps so, but then nowhere in the West is there free medical treatment and compulsory education up to the age of eighteen, as there is here. And they didn't even know what it was to be at war, while we fought for them and the whole of Europe. Instead of defending their homeland, they prefer to make money. And you, sir, are mistaken,' this to Jozef, 'the Comrade Secretary was referring to them when he said that there are people without a homeland.'

Jozef did not protest. He was uncomfortable, hot, and very thirsty.

But Maryla could not hold back, 'The Comrade Secretary was talking about two homelands, I'm sure it was two, about the Zionist one and the patriotic one.'

When she said this, the Critic jumped up and tried to interrupt her, but Maryla went on, '... and the Comrade Secretary proposed that all of them should choose one

121

of these homelands, and in this way the principles of our democracy would be fulfilled.'

'The young lady is right,' added the fat man. 'We were once a homeland of two nations, but the economic and political situation now does not allow it,' and the fat man began giggling and shaking his sweaty bald head.

The man in the corner who had been covered by his newspaper the whole time, stirred restlessly but was still again a moment later.

'Obviously,' the officer took up the subject, 'we are finally a nationally homogeneous country without national minorities and the problems connected with them, and only the citizens of Jewish origin, who now have their own homeland, still have to decide.'

'Decide on what?' asked the young man.

'On emigrating, of course,' answered the officer.

And little Jozek, who for the whole journey had been sleeping with his head resting on Jozef's shoulder, dreamed that his father said to his mother, 'We won't be moving, Rachel. I've withdrawn the deposit and we'll stay put. Let the Mazurkiewiczes clear out with their little brat, Heniek, if my Jewish child disturbs him.'

Chapter 15
CALIFORNIA

Maryla was not at home, as she had gone to the beach to sunbathe, so Jozef was left by himself. He had no wish either to make his bed or to have breakfast. He turned off the radio as it was getting on his nerves, and was just about to phone Rabinowicz but the Critic came in and said, 'In this matter, my dear colleague, just the two of us must decide and nobody else.'

And Jozef replaced the receiver.

'I don't like butting into grown-up matters,' said little Jozek, who had just run into the room, 'but if you want me to, I'll also tell you what I think of it.'

Jozef was very pleased that little Jozek had come in, and the Critic, as always, was extremely annoyed.

'We cannot make any childish decisions,' he said. 'They are either naive or one-sided. The matter is too complex and requires the Party approach, and you are still too young and...'

'I'm not as young as all that,' Jozek said indignantly. 'And anyway, one doesn't have to be a grown-up to know what the Party is. As you know, sir, I've been taking Latin at school for a year now. I also know the word "approach". It can be wrong or it can be right, and if you can tell me which is the Party one, then I will be able to join in your discussion,' and Jozek made himself look very serious.

'All right, Jozek, said big Jozef. 'Then listen to what I and my colleague the Critic have to say to each other.'

'Let's start from the very beginning,' the Critic began. He had now come to terms with Jozek being present, as he had no option. 'The Comrade Secretary has entrusted to both of us some very responsible tasks.'

'What tasks?' asked Jozek.

'I will explain it all to you,' Jozef lit a cigarette. 'You see, at Party House there is a commission at work investigating the question of our people's participation in rescuing Jews from extermination. And the Comrade Secretary has asked me to join this commission.'

'I understand,' said Jozek, and after a little thought he added, 'You've already told me all about the war, and the Germans, and that they killed Jews because they were anti-Semitic. But what I don't really understand is how the Germans knew who was a Jew. Surely it was possible to change your name, like you did. If my name were not Hirszfeld, then nobody in my class or in my yard would know that I was a Jew. Although...' and Jozek reflected again. 'Although,' he went on, 'they had

124

'... The job of this second commission is to detect Zionists
who are harming our Party' (page 126)

another way of finding out, that's true, but if Heniek hadn't pulled down my shorts...'

'Well, there you are,' Jozef interrupted. 'The Germans did the same.'

'O.K.,' said Jozek, 'but they couldn't really do that to everybody...'

'They could and they did,' the Critic stated conclusively.

'I can't really believe that,' Jozek replied, 'and I'm sure they didn't identify girls that way.'

Jozef laughed, and the Critic bit his lips in anger, for he was very sensitive to the immoral utterances of the young, and particularly children.

'... From which we can draw the conclusion,' Jozek went on, as if he were speaking at a meeting of his Class Council, 'that somebody helped the Germans in finding the Jews!'

'Let's end this senseless conversation,' the Critic was irritated, 'because it's not leading us anywhere,' and he wanted to leave.

'Please don't upset yourself, my dear colleague,' said Jozef and he stopped the Critic. 'And you, Jozek, listen now and don't interrupt. As I have already told you, the Comrade Secretary has invited me to join this commission which is to work under the Chairmanship of Major Mazurkiewicz. The job of this second commission is to detect Zionists who are harming our Party.'

'Not so fast,' said Jozek, 'because I don't understand any more. Please explain to me in what way the Zionists are harming the Party. I heard and so did you from Rabinowicz, that Zionists are patriots and that the Party is also...'

'This Rabinowicz,' put in the Critic, 'is a hostile element.'

'Please don't interrupt, dear colleague,' said Jozef,

and he turned to Jozek. 'Listen. The Zionists are patriots of their own country, but not of ours. Do you understand?'

'Not really,' answered Jozek. 'Because if they are patriots of their own country, and we of ours, then we should be friends and not enemies, and we should not be fighting each other. After all, they didn't declare and wage war against us, but against the Arabs.'

'But we, you young whipper-snapper,' shouted the Critic, 'are on the side of the Arab nations, and not on that of the aggressor.'

'Now I understand everything,' said Jozek. 'Only I am not on the side of the Arabs, and I'm sure that Jozef isn't either.'

'In that case,' screamed the Critic, 'you are against us!'

'Not at all,' replied Jozek calmly, which irritated the Critic even more. 'I'll give you a simple example. Our class is split into two camps. One side supports the "Pogon" and the other the "Ruch" team. I support the "Pogon", but that doesn't mean that I am an enemy of Antek who supports the "Ruch". As for Goldberg, he supports "Hasmonea", although it hasn't even been placed in the National League. It's true, of course, we do argue among ourselves a bit, but we are in the Class Council together, consult together, and the class listens to us. Now why don't you grown-ups do the same in your Party?'

Jozef laughed again, but the Critic shook with anger.

'Calm down, now, calm down,' said Jozef. 'Let me go on. Now we two, that is to say, my colleague the Critic and myself, as members of both of these commissions should co-operate with each other very closely and help each other out.'

'Help each other out in what?' asked Jozek.

'Myself,' answered Jozef, 'in unmasking Zionists who

are hiding under false names, and my colleague the Critic in compiling a list of those brave people who should be given awards for saving Jews. And both of us will be applying our censure to those who were rescued, but who have forgotten their gratitude and now serve the Zionists.'

'I'm sorry,' said Jozek, 'but could you repeat that again? I didn't understand a thing!'

Jozef repeated everything in great detail and with great patience, and little Jozek listened.

'All right,' he said when Jozef had finished, 'but I'm very frightened that something might happen like what happened to our manuscript.'

'What are you talking about, Jozek?' Jozef asked. 'I don't see the connection. Or perhaps you haven't quite understood everything yet?'

'Oh, I understood all right,' said Jozek, 'and I thought to myself, if you are compiling a list of Zionists, that is to say, of Jews, since Rabinowicz said that only a Jew could be a Zionist, and if you write their real names on this list, then some anti-Semites like Heniek would steal that list, the way he stole our manuscript, then they would discover who is a Jew and would be able to persecute him. It's occurred to me in fact that the Germans probably had such a list and therefore knew who was a Jew and who was not.'

'This is too much!' exclaimed the Critic, and ran out of the room.

And little Jozek looked at big Jozef, who was very sad, and said, 'Let's go down to the beach, Maryla's waiting for us. We can have some ice cream on the way. I'll treat today, my mother gave me something for my good report.'

And off they went.

Maryla was sunbathing on a deck-chair and talking to the Professor, who was sitting next to her on a rubber mattress. Jozef and Jozek sat down next to the Professor and listened to what Maryla was saying.

'I don't understand, Professor, why you think we are badly off because we are ruled by others. I'm not too good on my history, but I was taught that, to bring some order into the country, they dragged in Jagiello from Lithuania and Batory from Hungary. I wouldn't say Bona the Italian was much of a hit here... Let's take Kazimierz the Great. Wasn't he the one who brought in the Jews, since without them he wouldn't have found the country built in wood and left it built in brick? My personal opinion is that it isn't so much Kazimierz as his Esther who deserves to be called 'the Great'.'

'You're exaggerating, Miss Maryla,' interrupted the Professor, who pretended that he was laughing, though the truth is that he was rather annoyed because he didn't like seeing history mocked.

'And what about old King Jan III, what did he do?' Maryla continued, 'He defeated the Turks and saved Christianity, all very well, but as a result left us constantly exposed to the wind from the West. The Turks would have gone without his help anyway, they never threatened us, and had they roughed up the Germans a little, which is what our Great King Jan did not allow them to do, then perhaps we would have had a little less Christianity and a little more peace. Or Wladyslaw. Instead of imprisoning the Shuyskys here, he'd have done better to stay in Moscow himself. No,' said Maryla, 'an eagle with a crown we certainly have had, but eagles on the throne we most definitely have lacked, and we lack them even now.'

'Who could have told you such nonsense?' enquired the Professor, now fuming with anger.

'I got to it myself with just a little bit of common sense, even though everyone seems to deny me that,'

129

Maryla chuckled because she liked to see the Professor annoyed.

'And what do you say to this?' the Professor turned to Jozef.

But Jozef had no desire for a discussion, which is why he said, 'I have no influence over her at all, dear Professor. If there is anyone whom she is prepared to believe, it can only be you.'

'That is only too true,' said Maryla. 'At least our Professor knows what he wants and knows his history better than you know your literature.'

The Professor was pleased when he heard this, for he calmed down and said to Jozef, 'That's how it is with our pretty young ladies and there's nothing that can be done about it.'

And Maryla winked at Jozek, took him by the hand, and they ran down to the river together.

The Professor lay down on the mattress, and Jozef in the deck-chair, and they both dozed off.

The Professor, who belonged to the same commission as Jozef, noticed all of a sudden that Jozef was slipping some important documents into his pocket. And Jozef noticed that the Professor, who appeared to be glancing over the list of Zionists, was surreptitiously writing Jozef's name on the list.

Maryla returned and brought with her an athlete, to whom she had promised some morello cherries in exchange for his having given her a ride in his kayak. She chased Jozef out of the deck-chair, told the athlete to sit down on the mattress next to the Professor, and handed him a bag full of cherry stones, having forgotten that she had already eaten the morello cherries herself. But the athlete was not in the least offended, he only asked if by any chance she had anything more substantial for him to consume. Maryla gave him some cucumber sandwiches, a hard-boiled egg, and some salt wrapped in a piece of paper.

'Priekrasno,' the athlete said and cracked the egg against the Professor's knee.

'Can you speak Russian?' asked the Professor because he had to say something and, for Maryla's sake, could hardly explode at the athlete's rather inelegant manners.

'Niemnozhko,' answered the athlete, and he stuffed the whole egg into his mouth. And when he had swallowed the egg, he added, 'I've been to Kiev for the Games, and, if I hadn't been prevented by circumstances beyond my control, I'd have chosen freedom, as the pay is much better there than here.'

'I've heard,' said the Professor, 'that with them sport is an amateur activity, that only non-professionals perform.'

'But professionals in making money, wouldn't you say?' asked the athlete.

'I don't fully understand,' said the Professor.

'There is nothing to understand. You sign a man up as an engineer, for instance. He goes to collect his pay once every three months, or they may even send him the money at his address by post, and all he does himself is train at a camp where he gets lush state keep. It's the same thing here, except they don't pay as much.'

'What do you mean,' asked Maryla, 'by circumstances beyond your control?'

'That cosmopolitans aren't popular there,' the athlete replied and bit into the cucumber sandwich.

'Cosmopolitans?' Maryla asked.

'You know, the people who change their homeland. To change your homeland, I mean from a Western one, of course, not from one like ours, into their Soviet one, is a privilege reserved only for the atom-shchicks, not for athletes. Do you get it?' and the athlete rolled

131

on to his stomach, lifted his legs into the air, and did a handstand.

'What are the atom-shchicks?' Maryla asked the Professor.

'Atomic scientists,' the Professor explained and hastily drew himself aside as the athlete nearly collapsed on top of him.

'And what are they doing with their Jews?' Maryla continued with her questions.

'What should they be doing?' the athlete asked in surprise and looked a little suspiciously at Maryla.

'I was only asking,' said Maryla, 'because the Professor... oh, I'm sorry, you gentlemen haven't been introduced...'

The athlete stretched out his hand to the Professor who offered him his own.

'... I was asking,' Maryla repeated, 'because the Professor maintains that they are exporting Jews to us so that these Jews can rule us.'

'I don't know anything about politics,' the athlete replied gravely, keeping Maryla and the Professor under careful alternating observation. 'It's not my field.'

'My dear young lady, you are simplifying the issue,' said the Professor, 'and that is not very nice.'

'I'm not simplifying it at all, that's exactly what you said,' Maryla defended herself. 'But never mind.' And she asked, 'Why are you staring at me like that?'

'Because,' said the athlete, 'ever since I found out that I was a Jew, everyone has reproached me for it.'

The Professor laughed, and Maryla whispered, 'I'm very sorry, I didn't mean to offend you.'

'Well, I must go,' said the athlete. 'I've got to be off, they're waiting for me.'

And he ran off.

'I'm a pig,' said Maryla.

And the Professor, obviously very pleased about something, launched himself into the following discourse:

'Please take note, my dear young lady, of their psychological grievances. The very word "Jew" gives rise in them to a reaction which cannot be observed in any other nationality. They feel relaxed, very sure of themselves, even, to put it frankly, insolent, as long as we treat them as one of us and don't find them out. Their reaction is proof of an inner self-exclusion, that's it, of the historical phenomenon of psychological alienation...'

'And whose fault is that?' interrupted Maryla. 'Kazimierz the Great invited them here so that they could live together with us, so that they could find a joint home with us, and we treat them like guests who have overstayed their welcome too long and have forgotten to clear out. Isn't that so, Professor?'

'Not quite,' said the Professor. 'To have a right to a home, one must have affection for that home. We love our country, we even love it as it is now, and that is why we have a perfect right to live here, while they have always betrayed this home and served the conquerors. They are doing the same today.'

'Not just them,' Maryla interrupted again. 'Today... let's be honest with ourselves, everybody serves. Please don't be angry with me, Professor, but you as well...'

Maryla stopped, for the leaf which she had stuck to her nose had just fallen off.

'That's not true,' said the Professor. 'First and foremost, I am contributing to the cultivation, and hence to the survival of our national values, so that they can endure all the occupying powers and their servants of foreign origin. I do this as an historian. Secondly, as a statesman... or, in other words, as a patriot, as one for whom the independence of our country is the overriding final goal. I am completely aware that this goal cannot

133

be achieved as long as a foreign body remains within our national organism. When we get rid of it, when our organism is restored to perfect health, then we will be able to deal with the occupier without any difficulty whatsoever, as we have done before in our history. Only a monolithic nation is strong enough to drive the occupier out, achieve co-existence and even partnership. That is why we must, oh yes, we must,' the Professor was becoming very agitated, which hardly ever happened to him, 'get rid of the Jews! My dear Miss Maryla,' the Professor was attempting to smile, so as to overcome his excitement, 'my dear Miss Maryla, I would like to be completely frank with you. There is much talk here of the Zionist Peril. In reality this is absurd. Zionism is no menace to us. On the contrary, if all Jews were Zionists and were to return to their historical homeland, they would only gain our deepest respect. There is no Zionist Peril, but there is a Jewish Peril, yes, a Jewish one, and we should admit that openly. It is the Jews, not those who declare themselves as Zionists, but those who claim a right to another's home so as to be able to infect our national organism, while secretly, or even quite openly, serving the occupying powers and making it easy for them...'

The Professor, though quite agitated again, had to stop there, for Maryla called over an ice cream vendor, bought two ice creams, and woke up Jozef, while the Professor took up one of the sandwiches left by the athlete, for he did not eat ice cream because he suffered from indigestion.

Jozek ran up to them. He had been kicking a ball around and was very tired. He took what was left of the ice cream from Maryla, and they all began to get ready to go home, as the weather had become worse.

On the way, Maryla said, 'I'm beginning to believe

that I really am stupid, for I cannot tell the difference between a "must" and a "right".'

'And what's this all about?' asked Jozef. 'A new philosophy?'

'Philosophy, my foot,' Maryla stopped to hail a taxi, as she had no desire to go by tram. 'The Professor keeps talking about the right to a homeland, or as he says — a home. But I wonder if it's not so much a question of a right as of a "must".'

The Professor looked at Maryla with astonishment, but he did not interrupt her, and listened closely to what she was saying.

'... Take this boy as an example. He must be stuck with the parents he's got, for, of course, he was given no choice. It was even a must that he be born here and not in Spain — nobody consulted him. He is and must be a Jew even though he has absolutely no wish to be one. And when he tried to love and perhaps has loved what he must be stuck with, he is then told that he has no right to it. No, something must be wrong here.'

Jozef remained silent, and the Professor could not answer Maryla even though he intended to, for a taxi had just pulled up in front of them and, once they had moved off, it was no longer possible to exchange opinions on the subject of must and right, for the cab driver, who had been driving an empty vehicle before he picked up these fares, now had a great desire to talk. So he took advantage of the situation and began,

'You, as I can see, are intelligent people and will forgive a Dummkopf like me if I ask you something. How is it that I'm slaving away on two shifts, my joints are cracking from this turning and turning, and yet I still can't earn enough to live on. It's good my kids are grown-up now, and as for my late wife, nothing is due her from this world — only a candle and flowers on All

Souls'. I was a driver before the war as well. For this Jew who traded in paper, you know. He didn't pay badly – that I'll say for him, and he looked after the car, even though it didn't belong to him but to the firm – I think a Swedish or a Dutch firm, but that was a long time ago. I drove a bit under the Germans. Well, what is there to say? It was war, but I never was hungry. And now the State gives me a job, the State gives me a car, everything from the State, and so what? Of course, people say, if everything is State-owned, then everything is unowned – so poverty. But I don't think it's true. A pal of mine used to drive a State-owned car in the old days, you know, and he built himself a house. Which means that it all depends really on who runs the State. And when he isn't fit to rule, then you know... But our people are just a flock of stupid sheep and don't deserve any better. I'm sorry, if I've stepped on anyone's toes, you know – these days people are getting a little jumpy and run off to write a complaint for just about nothing. But what's that to me – there's no "must" to bury the truth. You, Miss, won't denounce me, and they,' he nodded in the direction of Jozef and the Professor, 'they're probably dreaming of California already. Well, there's one thing – dreams can't be grabbed by the State yet. They're private and you don't need the local council's permission to have them. And people say there's no freedom here...!'

Chapter 16
THE PRESS LIES

'Please, I beg you, don't do it,' said Jozef to little
Jozek. 'Not only can it cause some unnecessary trouble,
but also it wouldn't be hard to have an accident. Anyway, believe me, it's not at all interesting.'

'You sound just like my mother,' Jozek pouted. 'She's
afraid of everything too. She's always telling me, "Don't
go there, don't come here. Be careful. Look out," as if
I didn't have a mind of my own. I'll bet all my friends
have gone and I'm the only one at home. They'll be
saying that I'm a coward.'

'Participation in a hooligan brawl is not evidence of
courage,' argued Jozef.

'Why do you put it like that,' Jozek said angrily. 'You know very well that that isn't true. The students from the University have even put on white caps so they can be told apart from the hooligans. I'd really like to see. I promise you I won't step off the pavement. And if you want to, come with me.'

'No, Jozek, I don't want to have anything to do with it. There'll be quite enough onlookers there without us. Let's go down to work. I'm not quite sure you know the fifteenth chapter well enough. But anyway maybe you'd prefer to go on to the next?'

'No, it's best if I repeat the fifteenth. And you repeat the fourteenth.'

'How about if we repeat them all, right from the beginning?'

'Okay, but me first,' Jozek agreed.

And so the two of them, the Little One and the Big One, began to recite, alternately, the chapters of their story. Jozek repeated all the chapters with odd numbers, and Jozef those with even numbers. Then they changed around, and afterwards, when they had repeated the whole thing again, they began to test each other at random. Little Jozek would begin a fragment, never mind which one, from whatever chapter he chose, and big Jozef would complete it, and so on, alternately. It went perfectly. They had not forgotten a single word, not a single comma or full stop.

And when they grew tired, they had some scrambled eggs which Jozef prepared. They were very pleased with themselves.

'Now,' said Jozek, 'not even a hundred stinking Henieks can steal anything from us. They can look for that manuscript high and low, anywhere they like, and they won't find anything.'

'Not even an army of Mazurkiewiczes,' added Jozef,

'I did not speak at all,' Jozef replied unwillingly (page 142)

'even if they dug up the whole earth and pumped out all the rivers, could find our story, for they can't see into our heads. We've made them look like a bunch of fools, haven't we?'

'And whose idea was it, then?' Jozek asked proudly.

'Yours, of course, yours, Jozek. There's no manuscript but the story still exists.'

'Only, have you kept your word?' said Jozek, 'you haven't confided it to anyone?'

'No one in the whole world knows anything about it,' Jozef assured him, 'and no one will, except ourselves.'

'Not even Maryla? Not even the Critic?' Jozek asked suspiciously.

'Not even they, I swear,' Jozef pronounced solemnly and poured some tea into the glasses.

Little Jozek helped himself to his third cake and asked, 'Don't you have any more cakes?'

'No, but go ahead, I don't want any,' replied Jozef.

'I don't either, I'll leave it for Maryla,' and Jozek put the cheesecake back on the plate.

'She should have returned a long time ago,' said Jozef. 'I hope nothing's happened to her,' and he reached for a newspaper. 'Let's read this, Jozek, and see what they've written about these students brawls.'

'I don't want to read it,' Jozek grunted. 'The press lies!'

Big Jozef looked searchingly at little Jozek.

'Who told you that?' he asked. 'I suppose you've already been there and you're hiding it from me?'

Jozek was slightly crestfallen, hung his head and said quietly, 'Only for a moment, while I was on my way to see you.'

And he took out of his pocket a leaflet with the words, 'The press lies. Read "Tiny Tots" — the only paper that does not lie yet'.

Jozek took the leaflet, read it, and tore it into little

pieces, which he then piled up in an ashtray and burned.

'Had they found something like that on you, you'd have been expelled from school immediately...'

'I saw those slogans everywhere,' said Jozek, and he was a little angry with Jozef for destroying the leaflet. 'And they wouldn't have done anything to me because everyone knows about it. They all know it's true.'

Jozef was deep in thought and did not reply, but he put the newspaper aside.

And Maryla still had not returned.

'And why,' Jozek asked suddenly, 'do the papers write that the Zionists are stirring up our youth?'

'Because there are Zionists among the ringleaders,' Jozef replied, but a little uncertainly and without looking at Jozek.

'You're not telling the truth,' said Jozek. 'I know the University students want the theatre to put on "The Forefathers' Eve" by Adam Mickiewicz, and they're not in the least against the Arabs.'

'It's not quite like that,' answered Jozef.

'Oh yes, I've wanted to ask you this for a long time, but I keep forgetting,' Jozek said. 'Is it true that I'm related to Mickiewicz?'

'You? I don't understand?' Jozef was puzzled.

'Because my grandfather,' replied Jozek, 'was also named Mickiewicz, Israel Mickiewicz.'

'That's just a coincidence,' Jozef laughed. 'It just happens to be the same surname. A lot of Jews born where Mickiewicz was born have the same surname.'

'Then maybe that's why,' Jozek continued his questioning, 'they're accusing the students of Zionism?'

'You're talking nonsense, Jozek, there's no connection.'

'Or maybe it's because,' Jozek continued to ask, 'Adam Mickiewicz, I've read this somewhere but I can't remember where, because Adam Mickiewicz created a

Jewish Legion? Do you know anything about that?'

Jozef laughed again, but he did not reply. Instead, he started pacing the room in agitation because Maryla had not yet come back.

Little Jozek could not restrain himself and cut off half the cake he had left for Maryla.

'You promised me,' he said, 'that you'd tell me what happened at the meeting of the Union.'

'Nothing of interest,' replied Jozef.

'And did you speak for or against?' asked Jozek.

'I did not speak at all,' Jozef replied unwillingly.

'And the Critic?' Jozek continued.

'The Critic spoke against.'

'Against putting on Mickiewicz's "Forefathers", yes?' Jozek insisted.

And when Jozef did not reply, little Jozek added contemptuously, '... That Critic is the biggest coward I've ever met. I wouldn't be a bit surprised if it turned out that he was a Jew. Tell me, why are Jews so cowardly?'

'That's not true,' said Jozef. 'Take Israel for example.'

'In Israel, it's not too hard,' said Jozek. 'They've got a good army...'

'Well, there you are,' Jozef interrupted him. 'When you don't have an army, you can't be brave.'

The telephone rang. It was the Professor asking about Maryla. Jozef said that she hadn't come back yet and that he was very worried.

It was getting late, little Jozek lay down on the bed, and Jozef stretched out beside him fully clothed. They couldn't sleep, because they were very upset that Maryla had not yet returned.

Towards morning Jozef said to Maryla:

'Come on, let's go for a short walk, I've got a bad headache.'

They walked across some lawns, and all about them

was greyish, as it was already dusk. Then they came out into a well-lit square, which was nearly empty, and walked up on to a railway bridge. Below them lay great piles of scrap iron and extinguished furnaces possibly for baking clay.

'I'm not going any further,' said Maryla and put a white cap on her head and took a catapult out of her pocket. 'I'll wait here for a taxi.'

'There aren't any taxis here,' answered Jozef and led Maryla down by a spiral staircase.

They came out into the square again, and approached a stone chair in which sat... Jozef had no time to tell who was sitting in this chair because Maryla suddenly began to scatter leaflets bearing the six-pointed star of Zion, and Jozef became so frightened that he started to run away. He turned round and saw that Maryla was running after him. He seized her hand and asked, 'Who was that man?'

'Adam Mickiewicz,' said Maryla. 'Look what he gave me.'

Maryla took a cuckoo out of her handbag, the same one that had been so bored while sitting in the broken clock.

'What do you need that for?' asked Jozef.

'It's asked me to take it with me when I leave, and in return it has promised to cuckoo out the whole of your manuscript,' and Maryla began to laugh very loudly.

Then someone seized Jozef's hands from behind, twisted them, and put him in a full nelson.

'I've got you,' shouted Major Mazurkiewicz, 'you infernal Zionist! I saw you scattering those leaflets under the statue of the National Poet!'

Maryla went on laughing, then she pulled back her catapult and fired a stone.

Jozef felt the stone hit him painfully in the forehead,

but he did not fall. Instead, Major Mazurkiewicz toppled headlong face down on to the ground, and little Heniek began to run away...

Jozef awoke with a start, sat up in bed, and for a long time could not understand where he was. He saw little Jozek who was sleeping by the wall on the bed, and he heard a loud knocking at the door.

He got up, opened the door and saw the concierge, who had brought some men with him.

They greeted Jozef very politely, apologized that their duty obliged them to come at such an early hour, and said that Major Mazurkiewicz also apologized profusely for this sudden invasion of a writer's home, but that it was necessary for the case that a check be made on Maryla's belongings.

The search did not last long, but the men were not very interested in Maryla's belongings, rather, they scrutinized Jozef's books and drawers.

Little Jozek continued to sleep and nobody disturbed him. One of Major Mazurkiewicz's men did in fact slide his hand underneath the mattress, but he did it very delicately so as not to awaken the child. He had a little kid like that too, he said, and in fact he was very fond of children in general, 'the flowers of our future' as he poetically expressed it because he was a specialist in literature.

They took leave of him very politely as well, but to Jozef's question concerning the whereabouts of Maryla they gave no reply.

Then the Critic came in and was a little surprised to see the room in such a mess. He saw little Jozek who was still asleep, and said, 'Well, of course, it's obvious, it's all due to that youngster. I've asked you so many times, my dear colleague, and yet you've been as stubborn as a mule.'

144

As for Maryla, the Critic explained that she was probably under arrest, and that it would be best not to phone the Major about the matter.

'... The most important thing,' added the Critic, 'is that they didn't find the manuscript. As for myself, I would advise you to make your way immediately to Party House, surrender the story of your own free will, and show contrition. I was there yesterday and appended my signature to a letter of protest against the occupation of Arab territories and the tortures which the Israelis are perpetrating against an unarmed population. I advise you to do likewise.'

And he started cutting bread for breakfast, even though it was now lunch-time.

Jozef began to help him, little Jozek got up, and they sat down together to eat.

'What can they do to Maryla?' asked Jozef.

'I only know this much that they arrested a large number of people suspected of participation in the street riots,' said the Critic, and he spread margarine over his slice of bread; he never ate butter.

'Perhaps the Professor will be able to help us?' Jozef asked.

'I would advise you not to concern yourself with this case. Your interest could give rise to suspicion,' said the Critic. 'Maryla is an adult and should be responsible for herself. Besides, if she is innocent, she will be freed. We live in a law-abiding country, my dear colleague. One should not forget that, and one should not allow oneself to be subjected to the provocative rumours spread by our enemies.'

Jozek was listening to this conversation, and said nothing.

Chapter 17
THE PROMISE

'How are you, old friend,' said the Bearded Chairman on the telephone to Jozef, as was his custom, but today he did not even ask 'how are things?' Instead, he informed Jozef in a very terse manner that he was to come to him at once about a very important matter, and that he was to bring little Jozek with him, those were his very words. He added that he would wait but, all the same, they should not delay, and he put down the receiver.

Jozef and little Jozek got into a taxi and went to the Union. While they were on the stairs to the second floor,

'... the reason for our meeting today is our interest
in your literary work...' (page 148)

Jozef was approached by the Not Unattractive Secretary who, after looking around to make sure that no one could see them, whispered in Jozef's ear, 'I've got something important to tell you, sir, please drop in and see me, best when I'm at home in the evening, only please don't phone,' and she walked off quickly before Jozef had time to say good-bye.

The Bearded Chairman was seated behind his desk in his office, and in front of the desk, at a small round table, sat two elegant gentlemen. When they saw Jozef, all three stood up and bowed politely, but they did not shake hands, after which the Bearded Chairman said, 'I won't be interrupting you, gentlemen,' and walked out closing the door behind him.

Jozef sat down on a chair by the small table with the two gentlemen, and Jozek in a soft armchair beside the desk.

'It is a great pleasure for us,' said the first one, seated on the right, 'that you were able to come and talk with us.'

'And, as I am sure you have guessed,' added the second, 'the reason for our meeting today is our interest in your literary work, especially your latest story...' he stopped for a moment, looked first at Jozef, then at little Jozek, and concluded, 'your joint story.'

'Well, for the time being,' answered Jozef, pretending to be a little abashed, 'I won't really,' he corrected himself, 'we won't really be able to say much about our story, as it is not yet finished.'

'As far as we know,' said the first, 'you already have fifteen chapters ready.'

'Sixteen,' corrected Jozef and noticed that little Jozek had given him a disapproving sideways glance.

Jozef felt a little silly that he was babbling unnecessarily instead of listening to what the others wanted from him, so he added, '... They are in fact very short chapters, and barely form part of the story.'

'And they are not quite ready yet,' added little Jozek.

'That does not matter,' said the second. 'Major Mazurkiewicz,' here he paused and leaned over to Jozef, 'would very much like to remind you of your promise, remember?'

Jozef was a little confused and did not know what to answer, but he was rescued from his quandary by little Jozek. He knew these tricks. When the teacher wanted to drag something out of his boys, he would always say that they had promised him something or other, although nobody would have been so stupid as to promise anything of the sort, unless there were no other way out. Which is why Jozek said, 'I never promised the Major anything, and I couldn't have because the story is not yet ready. And half...' he wanted to say 'composition,' but corrected himself and said '... a story is senseless to show.'

Big Jozef, however, instead of aligning himself with little Jozek, said, 'You see, Jozek, but I really did promise, only I...'

'Only,' interrupted little Jozek, who was getting a little angry with the Big One, 'the story has not yet been written.'

'What do you mean, not yet written?' the second asked in surprise. 'But it was written. As far as we know, the manuscript...'

'The manuscript has been burned,' little Jozek quickly stepped in, worried that big Jozef might say something stupid again.

'Burned?' said the first one astonished. 'But you yourself said,' here he turned to Jozef, 'that there are sixteen chapters ready.'

And little Jozek butted in again. 'Ready,' he said,

'means thought out, not written down.'

The first looked at the second, and the second at the first, and they were silent for a moment.

'In that case,' said the second, 'at Major Mazurkiewicz's request, we would ask you to write down what has been thought out and submit it to the Major.'

'That may take a little time,' said Jozef.

'It should not take long,' the first one said firmly.

'We can help you, gentlemen,' said the second, 'and provide you with all the necessary facilities.'

'Where would you, gentlemen, prefer to write,' asked the first, 'at home or with us?' and without waiting for a reply, he added, 'In three days' time we will await you, gentlemen, in Major Mazurkiewicz's office.'

They both got up, bowed politely, and left without shaking hands.

'Oh, I'm so happy,' Maryla shouted as she danced around the room, 'that I'm home at last.'

Jozef was happy as well, and even the Critic was a little less downcast than usual. Only little Jozek, though also pleased about Maryla's return, could not brush away certain unpleasant thoughts, so much so that he didn't even want to eat the superb cream rolls that big Jozef had bought for him and Maryla. And when Maryla had at last cried herself out with joy, he whispered to Jozef, 'We've got to discuss what we're going to do next.'

Jozef was not very anxious to discuss anything, nor was Maryla, but there was no getting away from it. Maryla began first.

'I suppose you think that I got myself arrested during some scuffle, or at the University, or some place scattering leaflets or setting fire to a cinema. Not at all, in fact I wasn't even arrested. I simply dropped into a shop to buy myself a white cap because they're the in-thing these days, but they had run out of caps, and I was about to leave when this really good-looking young man comes up to me, shows me his identity card, takes me ever so gently by the arm, leads me to his car, asking me to go with him... Where? Well, not for a drive because he is on duty, maybe some other time, Sunday, let's say, but to his boss, to his office, where they are waiting for me. And so they were. These two real creeps, they told me to sit down and sign the charge sheet, as they call it. Well, I signed it.'

'What did you sign?' asked Jozef.

'I told you, the charge sheet.'

'But what did it say?' Jozef insisted.

'That I'm being detained on suspicion of preparing subversive acts and the painting of the star of Zion on the statue of Adam Mickiewicz, which means that I was taking part in a hostile anti-State activity, or something like that.'

'And you signed that, Maryla?' the Critic asked amazed.

'Well, I had to. They told me that I had to sign it, which meant that I had acknowledged the charge.'

'Why didn't you say that it was untrue?' Jozef asked in astonishment.

'Well, obviously I said that, but they explained to me that the charge was correct, even if I had done nothing of the sort.'

'How do you mean "explained"?' Jozef could not contain his surprise.

'They said to me, "If you entered a shop with the intent to buy a white cap, that means you were preparing yourself to take part in a student demonstration which in legal language can be read as a subversive act because the demonstration was to take place illegally." I don't understand the law very well, but I'm sure they do.'

'And what about the star?' asked Jozek.

'Do you remember, Jozef, when we were supposed to go to the theatre, but you had a headache as usual and I had to go by myself? After the show, I went for a walk with Maczka and the Professor. We got as far as the statue of Mickiewicz where there were a lot of students. That geezer who was questioning me showed me a photo, with the statue daubed with a star, and with me, and a few other people next to me. "Do you recognize yourself?" he asked. I said yes because what else could I tell him. Fact is, I came out quite well in that photo. "That'll do," he said and wrote down my reply. "What'll do?" I asked him. "You have admitted the charge," he said. "No, I haven't," I said. "I was there, but I didn't even see that star, let alone paint it on." "All right," he said, "in that case I'll change the record. I'll write that you didn't do this yourself, but that you took part in it along with others." I didn't deny it because...'

'You're mad, Maryla!' Jozef and the Critic shouted together. 'You've behaved from start to finish like an idiot or a suicide.'

'Oh, you silly old big heads!' laughed Maryla. 'You indulge yourselves in literature, and yet you can't imagine a third possibility. I did not act like an idiot, or like a suicide. I acted like a person who is carving out a decent biography for herself.'

'Then what happened?' interrupted Jozef.

'Then,' said Maryla, 'they asked me about all the people I know, and all my friends from the Young Writers' Circle, where we meet, how we spend our time, and other rubbish like that. They asked me, and I told them, only I can't stop wondering why the hell they wanted to know.'

'And were they interested in me?' asked Jozef.

'Not then, not in you, the Critic, or Jozek.'

'Then when?' Jozef went on.

'Wait, not so fast. Well, when they had asked me about everything, and when I'd signed a load of papers, I asked how many years I was likely to get. And he said he didn't know, because only the court could decide that, but he supposed it would be at least three years, if not more.'

'And what happened next?' the Critic asked impatiently.

'Oh, nothing much. They put me behind bars and gave me a bowl of such horrible soup that all I could think of was how not to be sick while I was eating it, because I was very hungry. To stay three years would mean eating more than a thousand soups like that. No, that wasn't for me. I said to myself that it would be better to live without a biography and write an anti-novel than to cross out three years of my non-biographical life, and so I began demanding another interrogation. And then they began asking me all the same questions, but this time I denied everything. They didn't get angry at me, only when I asked if I could go home now, they said no, because it would depend not on them, but on the court which would decide when I had told the truth, the first time or the second, and then they locked me up again. I cried all night and all day and I didn't eat anything, it was so vile... and the bed was hard and you aren't allowed to lie on it during the day, only sit on a stool. Then another guy came in and said that they would let me go if I talked you into handing the manuscript of your story over to him.'

'And what did you say?' asked Jozef.

'What could I say? I said that you would definitely agree because you wouldn't want me to stay here, I even signed a paper for him. Then he chatted with me, very kindly...'

'What did you talk about?' Jozef asked, now very agitated.

'What should we talk about but your story. I even told him a few fragments from it and...'

'What fragments?' Jozef could not stop himself from exclaiming.

'Oh, various ones, for instance about that dream...'

'Which dream?' Jozef was no longer in control of himself.

'Oh, the one where you dreamed that I had placed a bomb under the desk of the Secretary at Party House, but the bomb did not go off because Major Mazurkiewicz found it first.'

'Oh, my God!' moaned Jozef and clutched his head.

'This is the end, the end,' the Critic murmured to himself. 'And yet I warned you, I warned...'

They sat like that late into the night.

And when little Jozek at last fell asleep exhausted, he dreamed that he was talking with his grandfather, Israel Mickiewicz. But what it was they talked about, Jozek could not remember, and even if he did remember, he would not have told Jozef, for Jozef had broken his word of honour and had babbled out everything in the story to that chatterbox Maryla.

Chapter 18
TIME ARRESTED

He received them very politely, asked them to be seated, 'over here', offering Jozef a chair on the right side of the desk and Jozek one on the left side, so that they sat opposite each other while he observed them from behind his desk.

In the corner of the room just next to the window, there was another desk, but the person sitting at it had his back turned to the room and was only able to hear what was going on behind his back.

'If you, gentlemen, will allow me,' said the man who had greeted Jozef and Jozek so politely, 'I must complete a few necessary formalities. First we should establish your personal data.'

He asked each his surname, first name, year and place of birth, occupation and so on, first Jozef, then Jozek.

When he had written it all down, he put his ball-point pen aside, as he was perhaps a little tired, lit a cigarette, offered one to Jozef, apologized that he had no toffees for Jozek in place of a cigarette, and at last spoke.

'We invited you gentlemen here today,' (why 'we', why the plural, it was quite obvious that the man by the window was not in the least interested because he was reading something avidly), 'we invited you,' he repeated, 'in order to question you as witnesses in the matter of a concealed manuscript of which you gentlemen are the authors. Interrogation procedure requires,' he continued, 'that evidence be given by each witness separately and not in the presence of the second witness, in order to make communication between witnesses impossible during the interrogation. In your case, however, one of those being interrogated is still a minor and is therefore entitled to give his evidence in the presence of an adult. This person should be his teacher, guardian, or some other adult who does not appear in the case, but under no circumstances a second witness. Major Mazurkiewicz has nevertheless bowed to your request and has allowed you gentlemen to give your evidence jointly, as he understands quite well that it is difficult for true friends to be parted even for an instant.'

Jozef was very perplexed when he heard this, as he had never requested anything, nor could he have requested anything, of Major Mazurkiewicz, as the first and last time he had seen him had been that occasion in the restaurant, but he pretended that he was not perplexed at all.

And little Jozek gave Jozef a black look, more out of anger than surprise, for he had suspected that Jozef

... and that working clocks were now the exception (page 159)

had concealed some deal from him again, this time — and this was something that he had not expected from Jozef — with Mazurkiewicz himself.

In the meantime, the man behind the desk continued. '... There is only one uncompleted formality now: are you gentlemen related to each other or not? For if you are related, you have a right to withhold evidence against each other, but if you are not related, you are not entitled to that right.'

Jozef reflected for a moment and then said, 'I am Jozef Potoczek, that is to say, the person who grew out of Jozek Hirszfeld.'

'And I,' said Jozek, 'I am Jozek Hirszfeld, who grew into Jozef Potoczek.'

When they had said this, they noticed that the man behind the desk had become red with anger, that it would take very little more to make him start shouting at them because he thought they were making fun of him. But he did not shout, he didn't get the chance, for the man with his back to the room said very quietly, 'Write it down as they say.' And just as quietly, but enunciating nearly every syllable, he added, 'Time has been arrested.' And he repeated 'arrested', as if he were afraid that the other might not understand.

But he understood at once, for even though he was still red with anger, he was already trying to smile at the two Jozefs.

Little Jozek just sat there as if nothing had happened, but big Jozef was so astounded when he heard 'Time has been arrested' that his mouth gaped open.

Oh, how naive grown-ups are, particularly if they are writers. Always wanting to amaze their readers with something, and so always searching for something new. They take great pains over not so much what they write as how they write it, to make it as original and as odd in form as possible. For instance, they fiddle with clocks and arrest time, as Jozef did, and are happy that no one else has ever come up with such an idea before.

True enough, Jozef did discover that Major Mazurkiewicz had also put his clock out of order, for otherwise Heniek could not have found the manuscript in Satan's kennel, but it had not entered his head that what he had considered most original in his story was not original at all, but normal and banal, and that working clocks were now the exception. Jozef had become so involved with his new literary form, he was so proud of it, that he did not notice when all clocks were stopped — those of the Party, those of the State, those of the co-operatives and, strangest of all, even some of the wrist-watches which were still in private hands. And it was a good thing that he had not noticed this, too, for otherwise it would have been such a terrible blow to him that it probably would have knocked him completely, for it is a well-known fact that, above all else, even above themselves, writers love their creative work, and especially its form.

The man behind the desk was still writing something down, and had even stopped being red, when the telephone rang. Someone was summoning both him and his colleague who had been sitting with his back to the room. So, both of them left immediately, and in their place came another person, whom Jozef and Jozek recognized as one of the pleasant men who had spoken with them in the Union.

'Well, my dear authors,' he said, 'I hope that I can report to the Major about your successful literary effort, and present him with your manuscript. It must surely be ready now.'

'Unfortunately,' said Jozef, 'we have not had the time...'

'We do not intend to write it,' interrupted Jozek.

'For the time being,' Jozef corrected. 'For the time

being we don't intend to,' he repeated.

'Ah, well,' said the man who had come from the Major, 'everyone has a right to possess his own thoughts and no one should force him to reveal them. However...' here he paused and looked at Jozef, 'such a man cannot be a writer in the service of our Party, which is what you hold yourself out to be. Well! I'll go further and say that thoughts which are concealed from our Party and from our nation are usually materialized in a manner detrimental to the Party and the nation, otherwise they would not be concealed. You surely would agree with that?'

Jozef did not know how to reply, for the argument was obvious and could not be refuted. So he remained silent, and little Jozek asked unexpectedly, 'And so you think that we should write this manuscript?'

'I cannot suggest anything to you, gentlemen,' came the reply. 'I would only wish to add that to be honest is a duty. If one keeps anything whatsoever secret from the Party and the nation, that means one has no confidence in them, that he considers them alien...' he paused once more, 'and then,' he continued, 'one should admit that honestly and abandon the community which one considers alien. That should be obvious.'

He stood up and left without waiting for an answer.

The other two came back and took their old places, one behind the desk opposite the Jozefs, the other by the window with his back towards the room as before.

'Gentlemen, you may go home,' said the man behind the desk. 'The interrogation is over. If you are needed, we,' he spoke in the plural again, 'will summon you.'

'I thought they would arrest us,' said Jozef to Jozek as they came out on to the street.

'And what would they have gained from that?' said Jozek. 'You heard what he said. They don't need us.'

They hailed a taxi and Jozef asked to be taken first to the grey tenement, where he left little Jozek, and then to the Not Unattractive Secretary.

'Oh, you've come at last, Mr. Potoczek, and I thought you had forgotten me,' she greeted Jozef, and asked what he would like to drink — coffee, tea, or cognac perhaps?

'Cognac,' said Jozef and sat down in the soft armchair.

'Had you stopped to think a little longer,' said the Not Unattractive Secretary,' about whether to come to me or not, you might not have found me here.'

'What do you mean, "not found"?' asked Jozef.

'Quite simple really,' she replied, 'I'm leaving.'

'You're leaving?' Jozef could hardly believe his ears. 'But you are not...'

'That's true, I'm not Jewish, but your friend, Rabinowicz...'

'Rabinowicz?!' Jozef nearly shouted in his amazement.

'Why are you so surprised?' she asked. 'After all, there's nobody but you to thank for this stroke of luck. Rabinowicz came to the Union and asked for you. I said that you were ill and that you were going to a sanatorium, do you remember? But he didn't want to know anything, he just insisted that I give him your private address. He said, "I haven't seen him for years and I might not see him again because I'm leaving." Then I asked, sort of as a joke, if he was leaving alone, because if he was, he could take me with him. And he replied quite seriously, "Once good people used to save our lives, and now the roles have reversed, and it is our duty to repay our debt of gratitude. I'll take you with me," he said, "but it will cost you a bit. You can pay me when we get there, in dollars".'

Jozef listened as if enchanted. He drank his third glass of cognac and poured himself a fourth, and then he became aware of the regular ticking of the wall-clock. He began to listen.

'Are you surprised,' asked the Not Unattractive Secretary, 'that my clock hasn't been stopped?' and she laughed. 'There is no reason for my time to be stopped, as I'm almost gone. I've picked up my passport already.'

'Time stopped... time arrested,' repeated Jozef.

He began to understand everything.

'Time arrested by order...' the Not Unattractive Secretary took up the theme.

But Jozef interrupted her. 'By order of Major Mazurkiewicz,' he said.

'Major, my eye!' exclaimed the Not Unattractive Secretary. 'What's all this about the Major?! Only the naive believe that. Time has been arrested by the order of the Secretary at Party House. Surely you read his latest speech?'

'But why has it been arrested?' Jozef asked very gloomily, for he was completely deflated that his idea about the clock had turned out to be so banal.

'You ask me why?' the Not Unattractive Secretary did not cease to be amazed. 'Surely it is obvious — for questioning.'

'For questioning? I don't understand.'

'For questioning who is a Jew, of course.'

The Not Unattractive Secretary was even a little offended by Jozef's questions, because it seemed to her that Jozef understood everything and was just pretending he didn't because he didn't trust her.

Jozef only groaned, downed his fourth glass, and poured himself a fifth so as to empty that one in one gulp, something he had never done before because he didn't like to be drunk.

Jozef came out into the street, turned right in the direction of the tram stop and...

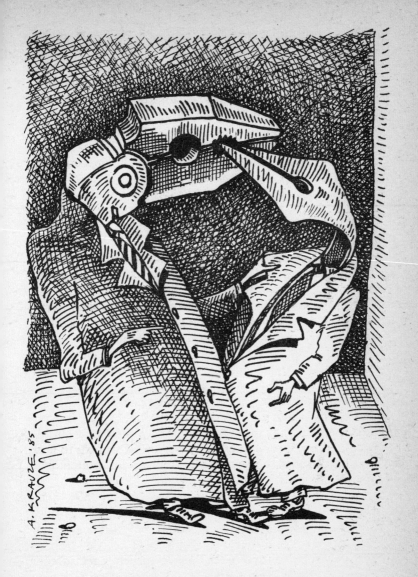

The first to speak was a delegate of the workers
from the agricultural machinery factory... (page 165)

'Good evening,' the Critic greeted him. 'Shall we go together?'

'And where are you going?' asked Jozef. 'Because I'll probably just go home.'

'Home?' asked the Critic in amazement. 'But today is the Party meeting, and our case is to be discussed. Had you forgotten by any chance, dear colleague?'

Jozef had forgotten. His head was in a whirl after the cognac and he wanted to sleep. And he was angry at the Critic for reminding him of the meeting, but he said, 'Well, in that case, let's go.'

They did not take a tram, as they still had about an hour to go, so they turned on to the boulevard. On the way Jozef entered a shop where he bought a packet of cigarettes, and the Critic an evening paper. They hardly exchanged a word, for what was there left to talk about? Only when they were approaching Party House did the Critic remark in a seemingly casual way, 'Please forgive me, my dear colleague, but I wish to be frank with you. If it comes to anything, you must understand that I will not be able to spare you. My Party membership card is, was, and always will be my most sacred possession. With you it is a different matter...'

'What are you talking about?' Jozef asked, but he did not really want to know what the Critic was talking about and was grateful that there was no reply.

In the waiting room outside the Secretary's office, where the Party Executive was now in session, a few people were sitting.

Jozef and the Critic sat down as well. They did not wait long, however. The door to the office opened slightly, and somebody whom they could not see properly, as the room was full of cigarette smoke, summoned them both to the meeting.

'And now, Comrades,' said the Chairman, 'we must

consider the question of the future presence in our ranks of Jozef Potoczek and his accomplice,' those were his very words, 'his accomplice,' he repeated, 'the Critic. In face of their joint,' he said 'joint', 'anti-Party position, we should consider their future membership in the Party jointly likewise. No objections?'

There were no objections, and the Chairman asked, 'Who wishes to speak?'

The first to speak was a delegate of the workers from the agricultural machinery factory who had been invited to the meeting. He stood up and said, 'And what is there left to discuss, Comrades? The matter is clear enough. The most dangerous enemy of all is the enemy in disguise who is ready to thrust his knife straight into our backs whenever he can. But nothing can be concealed from the eye of the ever-vigilant proletariat, not even anti-Party dreams, as enemies of the working class and of our nation may hope. As for the other one who pretends to be a critic, he covered his colleague cunningly, like a weasel, but he didn't quite cover him well enough. He kept quiet about that questionnaire because he thought the Party knew nothing. But what more is there to say? Let us not waste words. Chuck them both out of the Party and so much for them. Let them go to their kibbutz and not stink up our air.'

He said this and sat down. The next to speak was the representative of the Party press.

'I am quite surprised, and it is our own fault, Comrades, that up to now we have tolerated in our ranks such propagandists of Zionism, and who knows, perhaps they are paid agents as well...'

Jozef did not listen. He did not even notice that it was now the fourth speaker, who was succeded in turn by the fifth... He smoked a cigarette and, without knowing why, started to repeat in his memory various fragments from the chapters of his and Jozek's story. He felt as if he could hear the cuckoo's call and Satan's joyful bark greeting him in front of the kennel, when suddenly something attracted his attention, and he began to observe the person who was now speaking – it must surely have been about the seventh. If one were only to cover him with a newspaper, thought Jozef, then he would be the spitting image... but of course, it was the man from the train compartment... And Jozef began to listen...

'I myself was a witness,' he was saying, 'of the Jewish, my pardon, the Zionist agitation carried out by these traitors here present, in the compartment of a passenger train proceeding on a route from...'

'That's a lie!' shouted the Critic, who had been silent until now. 'This is slander! I insist that you withdraw...'

Everyone burst out laughing.

'That's enough,' said the Chairman. 'Jozef Potoczek and his accomplice the Critic are dismissed from the ranks of our Party by a unanimous resolution. We will adjourn for a ten minute break.'

Jozef and the Critic left. Someone approached them in the waiting room.

'Excuse me,' he said, 'I am an old member of the Party, I've seen a lot of injustices in my life, and I still have the courage, even in this situation, to intercede for comrades, if I am certain that they aren't guilty. I have the feeling that you have not been dealt with fairly. But I would like to be sure. Let's go to the lavatory, Comrades, and there we can check... just a simple formality, but I must be certain, after which I will do everything in my power to...'

Jozef and the Critic did not listen to any more, turned their backs very impolitely on the old comrade with honourable intentions, went down as quickly as

'... I won't be able to get home tonight,
as the last tram has long since gone' (page 168)

possible to the ground floor and out into the street.

They started home but got lost on the way and arrived outside the grey tenement. It was already dark and now very late, so the front doors were shut. They walked away and stopped around the corner from which they could see part of the wire netting fixed on top of the wall, and both of them, Jozef and the Critic, after looking around to make sure that no one could see them, began to pee. Around them all was empty and dark.

Then they walked in the direction of Satan's kennel, and Jozef said, 'I'll pay him a visit – maybe he'll let me stay the night. I won't be able to get home tonight, as the last tram has long since gone.'

'In that case,' replied the Critic, 'good night, dear colleague. I'll go on foot, for Satan wouldn't let me into his kennel.'

And he went away.

Satan, who had been wandering about in the garden, was overjoyed at Jozef's visit and even wanted to offer him a juicy bone, but Jozef politely refused. Nor did he have any particular desire to hold a conversation, so he lay down comfortably in the kennel, and fell asleep.

He dreamed first that the Professor had found him in the kennel and said, 'Please come with me, I'll hide you in the attic of my villa. You will be quite safe there. The sacred right of hospitality will preserve you from them, and when the war is over, you can return to your historic homeland...'

'No, thank you, sir,' Jozef replied, 'it would be best if I stay here with Satan.'

And Jozef woke up. After a while he fell asleep again and dreamed that everything that had happened until now – the broken clock, the story, the meeting at Party House and everything, everything else had only been a dream – a normal, silly dream.

168

Chapter 19
The next to last thought out by the authors, but, because it was uninteresting, forgotten.

Chapter 20
THE WELCOME

The express moved slowly at first, then faster and faster... The Critic sat next to a window, took the morning paper from his briefcase and spread it out, but he had no wish to read it. He closed his eyes in an attempt to blot out the station platform, with Jozef holding the arm of the weeping Maryla, little Jozek holding a barking Satan on a thick lead, the Bearded Poet puffing on his pipe, the Professor in a white hat, and a few other people waving their arms...

The express was picking up more and more speed, it ran into a dark tunnel, then jumped over a bridge, but neither the platform nor the people on it disappeared from view. They grew smaller and smaller, first to the size of gnomes, then to that of puppets, and they vanished from sight only when the express left the rail and soared upwards, dodging in and out of the grey clouds. The engine purred evenly and a very pretty stewardess approached the Critic and asked him quietly, 'Would you like coffee or tea, sir?'

'Coffee, please,' answered the Critic and he spread a white napkin over his lap.

The coffee was very good, even though it was instant, and the Critic asked for another cup.

The clouds parted and an unknown city could be discerned below... Suddenly someone shook the Critic by the arm. He started from his seat and nearly hit his head on the suitcase rack sticking out above him. He was no longer asleep. The wheels of the express were now turning on the rails, bumping a little...

'Please get ready for Customs Control,' he heard next to him.

An officer of the frontier guard shouted in his ear, 'Where to, sir?'

'Vienna,' replied the Critic.

'Your passport, please,' and the officer held out his hand.

The Critic reached into his pocket, took out his Party membership card and handed it over.

'This isn't the time for jokes, sir,' he heard.

And he felt all of a sudden that they had grabbed him by the arms and legs and were carrying him down the corridor. He heard someone's loud laugh. Maryla began to cry, and Satan leaped at him but did not hit him with his paw, only panted heavily... Someone opened the door of the hurtling express and the Critic tumbled down the railway embankment, straight into a ditch overgrown with tall grass...

'We are about to land. Please fasten your safety belts.'

The plane skipped a few times on the airport runway, and stopped. Someone opened the door and bright sun burst into the plane.

The Critic made his way down the steps from the plane. All around him there were people and flowers.

'We welcome you to your historic homeland!' said someone in a white shirt with a black skullcap on his head, who handed the Critic a microphone. 'Our radio listeners,' he said, 'would like to know what you felt when you finally stepped on to the land of your fore-fathers after so many, many years of wandering exile.'

The Critic stood upright, looked around at the white-clad people, and said, trying to speak straight into the microphone, 'Sisters and brothers! My dearest! Nobody could find words to express the deep emotion and that great, hitherto unknown joy, that real happiness...!'

The roar of another plane landing nearby with another group of happy arrivals drowned out the inspired words of the Critic.

'... I am grateful...' he tried to outshout the scream of the engines, 'I am extremely grateful,' he wanted to say 'to the Comrade Secretary from Party House', he wanted to shout out his name, and lifted his arm into the air to stress the greatness and nobility of the Comrade Secretary, but he stopped just in time.

The microphone began to jump, to swing like the pendulum of a grandfather clock, and the Critic was trying with great effort to remember the name of the local Comrade Secretary, his surname and his title, for surely it was necessary to say at last to whom he owed such gratitude. But he could not remember, no matter how he tried. The microphone disappeared and someone said, 'The readers of our newspaper would like to know if it is true that you were not allowed to take

'We welcome you to your historic homeland!' (page 172)

your furniture with you, and whether you believe in Communism with a human face?'

The Critic was about to reply, but another journalist shouted in his ear, 'Is it true that you had to work on the Sabbath and that you had your hat snatched off your head in the streets?'

'At long last!' sighed Maryla, and pushing the importune journalist aside, she embraced the Critic.

No, it was not Maryla. It was the Not Unattractive Secretary with Rabinowicz at her side. He is smiling at the Critic, winking at him, and after elbowing his way through the gaping crowd, he is leading him out on to a little square in front of a white pavilion. Here, a Fiat is waiting for them, and a few moments later they are flashing along an avenue of palm trees.

'And where is Jozef? and Maryla?' asks the Not Unattractive Secretary.

'My dear lady,' says the Critic, 'I would like to be frank with you, I can be frank now. No passport can make a man free. Freedom, and who could possibly know that better than yourself, Madam, must be achieved after a struggle. And they, and I am sorry to have to say this, they, Jozef, Maryla... you understand, they have never awakened to the salutary breath of freedom — they are not capable of it...'

'It's your turn now,' said the elderly lady to the Critic, who was sitting on a bench in the waiting room of the emigration office.

The Critic got up, took an envelope out of his briefcase, and gave it to the clerk in the window. The clerk took it, inspected the contents of the envelope, asked him to sign his application for permission to renounce his citizenship, and said, 'That is all. We will let you know.'